It was him. The man from the boatyard.

Chase.

What was he doing here? Earlier, Jemima had imagined herself glancing at him with cool confidence, but now that he was standing in front of her, she just wanted to run. But it was too late. As if feeling her scrutiny, he looked over and his gaze collided with hers.

"Hello again." He paused and she felt her stomach somersault as his green eyes locked with hers. "How's the bike?"

"I swapped it for a moped. The Italian one," she added.

"Is that right?"

She nodded. "I didn't get very good advice. Apparently the man who helped me didn't actually work at the Cycle Shack."

His smile widened and she felt her pulse accelerate. "I spend enough time there it feels like I do."

"But you don't."

"No, I don't," he agreed.

"Well, don't let me keep you from your game, Mr—" Lifting her drink, she looked pointedly past his shoulder.

"Just call me Chase."

He was trouble alright, she thought. *Chase.* It was what predators did, she thought, her brain spinning like a top. And this man was an apex predator.

Hot Winter Escapes

Sun, snow and sexy seductions...

Whether it's a trip to the Swiss Alps or a rendezvous on a gorgeous Hawaiian beach, warming up in front of the fire or basking in the sizzling sun, these billion-dollar getaways provide the perfect backdrops for even more scorching winter romances and passionately-ever-afters!

Escape to some winter sun in...

Bound by Her Baby Revelation by Cathy Williams

An Heir Made in Hawaii by Emmy Grayson

Claimed by the Crown Prince by Abby Green

One Forbidden Night in Paradise by Louise Fuller

And get cozy in these luxurious snowy hideaways...

A Nine-Month Deal with Her Husband
by Joss Wood

Snowbound with the Irresistible Sicilian
by Maya Blake

Undoing His Innocent Enemy
by Heidi Rice

In Bed with Her Billionaire Bodyguard
by Pippa Roscoe

All available now!

Louise Fuller

ONE FORBIDDEN NIGHT IN PARADISE

◆H HARLEQUIN
PRESENTS

Recycling programs
for this product may
not exist in your area.

ISBN-13: 978-1-335-59313-9

One Forbidden Night in Paradise

Copyright © 2023 by Louise Fuller

For questions and comments about the quality of this book,
please contact us at CustomerService@Harlequin.com.

Harlequin Enterprises ULC
22 Adelaide St. West, 41st Floor
Toronto, Ontario M5H 4E3, Canada
www.Harlequin.com

Printed in U.S.A.

Louise Fuller was a tomboy who hated pink and always wanted to be the prince—not the princess! Now she enjoys creating heroines who aren't pretty pushovers but are strong, believable women. Before writing for Harlequin, she studied literature and philosophy at university, then worked as a reporter on her local newspaper. She lives in Royal Tunbridge Wells with her impossibly handsome husband, Patrick, and their six children.

Books by Louise Fuller

Harlequin Presents

The Man She Should Have Married
Italian's Scandalous Marriage Plan
Beauty in the Billionaire's Bed
The Italian's Runaway Cinderella
Maid for the Greek's Ring
Their Dubai Marriage Makeover
Returning for His Ruthless Revenge
Her Diamond Deal with the CEO

Christmas with a Billionaire

The Christmas She Married the Playboy

Visit the Author Profile page
at Harlequin.com for more titles.

CHAPTER ONE

JEMIMA FRIDAY STEPPED off the plane at L. F. Wade International Airport in Bermuda into air that was as warm and soft as sun-dried bedsheets.

It was only seven hours and seventeen minutes since she'd left Heathrow Airport, but it felt as if she had arrived not just in a different country but on a different planet. Gone was the abrasive, cold grey London sky and in its place was a cloudless canopy of perfect aquamarine. Better still, the sun was shining.

But it wasn't just the sky that was lighter and brighter. Everyone making their way across the runway to the arrivals terminal was dressed in pastel colours, and they were smiling.

Her heart gave a wobble. She was a little low on smiles right now. She'd had to extend her overdraft again. Her PhD on 'accidental' reefs had lost its way and, to top it all, last week she came home to find her boyfriend, Nick, in bed with another woman.

She was still more than a little apprehensive about this, her first solo holiday. But despite her nervousness she had to admit that it wasn't a completely crazy idea

to get away from the scene of the crime and go somewhere the sun was shining and people smiled without
a reason. Maybe she might even find a reason to smile,
she thought as she made her way to passport control.
That holiday fling her sister Holly was so certain would
happen.

Although given her track record with men it seemed
highly improbable.

It felt like a hundred years since Holly and Ed had
suggested that she take a holiday but in fact it was two
days. At first she had been too stunned to react, but as
it sank in, she was appalled.

'I can't just up sticks and fly to the other side of the
world,' she'd protested when her siblings had turned up
at her cottage with a takeaway and tub of ice cream...

'Why not? And Bermuda isn't the other side of the
world. It's only seven hours away. That's about the same
time it would take to get to Inverness.' Ed had flopped
down on the sofa, then frowned. 'Did that bastard take
the TV?'

'What?' She had glanced across the room at the holes
in the wall where Nick had unscrewed the TV bracket.
It wasn't just the TV that had disappeared. Other things
were missing too. Nick's ratty bathrobe no longer hung
from the bedroom door and she didn't keep tripping
over his guitars. And there was a hollowed-out ache inside in her chest, although she could still feel her heart
beating, which surprised her as the rest of her felt numb
with shock and shame.

Her ribs seemed suddenly too tight.

Had she thought Nick was different from the other

men she had dated? In appearance maybe, but pretty much the first time they met she knew he was a mess. He was in a band but got paid in pints and he slept on other people's sofas. Only instead of running a mile she had started seeing him.

Holly and Ed had been appalled, of course, then resigned. He was, they agreed, exactly her type. Handsome, damaged, and destined to break her heart. But even though she knew they were right, she had wanted him. Or rather she had wanted to do what she had failed to do for her father. To fix him, to save him from himself.

Her breath caught in her throat as she pictured her father stumbling out of the pub, staring at her blearily as if she were a stranger and not his fifteen-year-old daughter. But you couldn't fix someone who didn't want to be fixed. It had taken a long time for that message to sink in, and finally she was done trying.

Done with tortured, unfixable men.

Done with men, full stop.

'Don't change the subject,' she had said, more to stop her brother railing against Nick's perfidious behaviour than because she wanted to discuss the twins' hare-brained scheme. Ed had already been eloquent on the matter and she didn't need to be reminded again of her ex's flaws or her stupidity in ignoring them. 'And it's obvious why not. I'm supposed to be finishing my PhD, not gallivanting off on holiday. Look, it's a lovely idea and I love you both for thinking of it, but I can't possibly—'

'But that's the thing—you can't not. You see, it's not

an idea…' Holly had given her a sheepish grin. 'It's a fact. We booked the flight.'

'And sorted out the accommodation,' Ed had added. 'You leave the day after tomorrow and, yes, I know it's short notice—' he had raised his hand up like a traffic policeman to stop the flow of her objections '—and, yes, we should have talked to you first but we knew if we gave you time to think you'd never do it.'

Holly had grabbed her hand and pulled her onto the sofa. 'I know you're worried about your PhD but you've been working on it for ten months now. Ten days isn't going to make a difference one way or another. Besides, you've always wanted to go to Bermuda and it's the perfect place to work.'

'If I'm going to work then I don't need to fly to Bermuda. Besides, they probably don't even have the Internet.'

Sensing weakness, Holly had grinned. 'Of course they do, Jem. I checked. And as you already know, they have over four hundred wrecks off the coast. So if you find some sexy sailor to take you out on his boat you can write it off as fieldwork.'

'And,' her brother had chipped in, 'you haven't had a holiday in years. Everyone needs a holiday, Jem, even you.'

A holiday.

The word had tasted like sherbet on her tongue and as expected she'd capitulated. When the twins stuck together they were almost impossible to unstick, and although the idea of travelling on her own to a distant and mysterious island made her pulse beat out of time, a part of her had felt almost relieved that she would be somewhere other than the cottage.

'Please, Jem. You need this. Just promise me that you'll go all in.' Reaching out, Holly had touched the blonde hair scraped into an unforgiving bun at the back of her head. 'Promise me that you'll let this down for once. And wear your contacts.'

'Okay, okay, I promise I'll let my hair down.'

'And have some fun.' Holly's blue eyes had gleamed. 'Have a fling. You're not just swapping homes, you're swapping lives.'

'You don't know anything about her. She could be a social outcast.'

'Then be someone else. It's just ten days, Jem. You can be anyone you want.'

And that was the difference between them. The twins were like their father. She was like hers. When life gave them lemons, they made lemonade. She never got that far because she was too busy worrying about the ratio of sugar and water. Or whether the lemons were ripe enough.

You can be anyone you want.

She glanced over at the luggage carousel, Holly's words replaying inside her head. Right now she'd settle for being that lucky person whose bag was the first to appear.

Incredibly, her suitcase was the first to appear. So far, so smooth, but she still had to find her way to Joan's beach house and she headed towards the exit, her nerves popping as she stepped into the sunlight again.

It was still strange to think that she would be living in someone else's house. Almost as strange as the idea of Joan living at Snowdrop Cottage. She bit into her lip. She'd only had one, snatched conversation with Joan Santos and she seemed fun and friendly, and Holly said she would drop round and say 'hi'. So stop worrying, she told herself. But that was easy to say, almost impossible to do. Worrying came as naturally to her as breathing. And taking an impromptu holiday on her own was well out of her comfort zone.

Only it was too late to think about that now.

There was a line of taxis waiting outside the airport and she approached the first in the queue trying to channel her younger sister's charm and her brother's unflappable calm.

'Where to?' the driver asked as he slid her bags into the boot of the car.

'Farrar's Cove, please. Do you know it?'

He nodded. 'Oh, I know it.' Slamming the boot, he grinned. 'Don't look so worried. It's beautiful. Very private and quiet. You pretty much got a whole beach to yourself. But if you get tired of quiet, just walk right on up the beach to the Green Door and you can dance until the sunrise.'

She leaned forward. 'The Green Door.'

'It's a bar.' His grin widened. 'It's raw Bermuda; you won't find many tourists but it's the best bar on the island. Best rum. Best music. And not just because my sister owns it.' She saw the driver grin in the rear-view mirror. 'Just ask for Aliana. She'll look after you. Tell her Sam sent you. That's me.'

'Nice to meet you, Sam, I'm Jemima, but most people

call me Jem.' She smiled. It was kind of Sam to look out for her but bars weren't her thing. She didn't drink, and as for dancing. Reaching up, she touched her bun. Letting her hair down was not something she did naturally.

Settling back against the warm leather upholstery, Jem stared through the window at the passing streets. Aside from the legendary triangle, and the namesake shorts, all she knew about Bermuda was that it was supposed to be the inspiration for the island in Shakespeare's *The Tempest*. But as they drove through the main town of Hamilton, she was more than a little surprised.

It was a pastel paradise. Everything was painted in soft pinks and yellows and blues. But mostly pink. It couldn't be any more different from England's grey cities and yet strangely there were old-fashioned British telephone boxes.

Just like the one Nick had pulled her into that first night they met when it was raining so hard. She had thought it was so romantic. A week later he'd told he was in love with her and moved into the cottage.

There had been no signs, nothing amiss when she let herself back into the cottage early. Music, some indie band that Nick loved and she tolerated, was playing loudly. And the cottage was swelteringly hot; she could remember feeling that familiar tic of irritation that Nick, who paid no bills, had no qualms about turning up the heating while she wore a coat and fingerless gloves and sat with a hot-water bottle to stop her body from cramping as she hunched over her laptop.

She hadn't called out his name. She had wanted to surprise him.

And she had.

A shiver of misery and humiliation pulsed across her skin as she remembered the moment when she stepped into the bedroom. At first, she hadn't quite taken it in, almost as if her brain was trying to protect her from what her eyes were seeing, only she couldn't not see it. See them. Nick, his handsome features blunted with desire; the woman's mouth an O of shock, their bodies shining with sweat in the pale afternoon light.

The woman had fled. Nick stayed. At first he was sulky and defensive, then accusatory, listing her faults, then finally he told her he was leaving. And that was that. Another failed relationship, another reminder of how she had failed to save her father from his demons.

For a moment, the shadows of the past seemed to creep into the taxi, and with an effort she pushed them away. While she was here in the sunshine, she was going to take a holiday from all the memories and regrets that crouched in the shadows.

Away from the town, the countryside was gentle but she kept getting tiny, teasing glimpses of pink sand and a sea that looked like blue glass. As he drove, Sam chatted about Bermy, as he called Bermuda, and by the time she felt the car slow, most of her nerves had faded away.

They had left the main road some five minutes earlier and now the road surface was getting rougher, and then the dunes parted and she felt her breath catch in her throat and before the car had even come to a stop she was opening the door and running towards a tiny pale green painted cottage.

When Joan had said it was 'compact' she hadn't been joking. But the sand touched the steps leading up to the veranda, and it was pink.

She blinked. There were palm trees too.

It could have come straight from the pages of *Robinson Crusoe*. It was perfect and she took a photo and sent it to Holly and Ed.

Inside was as tiny as it looked. Tinier even than her cottage at home. Just a bedroom, a miniature bathroom and living room with a kitchen at one end. There was a bowl of exotic-looking fruit on a doll's-house-sized table and tucked underneath was a piece of paper with her name on it.

Hi Jem,
Welcome to my home! Use whatever you want. I made up the bed fresh and the towels are brand new.
    Just a heads-up, my axe packed up yesterday and I didn't have time to get it fixed but you can hire one in Hamilton.
Have fun,
Joan x

Joan sounded so nice, she thought, staring wistfully down at the note. It was a pity she was never going to meet her. She frowned. Why would she need an axe though? And why would she need to hire one?

She turned towards where Sam was putting her bags by the door.

'Sam, do I have to chop wood for something? Only Joan says the axe is broken.'

He laughed. 'Axe is slang. She means her moped. That how you planning on getting around?'

Truthfully she hadn't got that far. It was one of the many things she hadn't had time to plan for. 'I suppose so. But don't I need to have a licence?'

He shook his head. 'Not if you're hiring one. The Cycle Shack is the place to go. It's down by the harbour. I'll drop you there on my way back to the airport.'

The Cycle Shack clearly did a whole lot more than hire out bikes and mopeds. It also sold hardware, fresh coffees and acted as a collection and drop-off point for post and parcels. And judging by the people milling around chatting and greeting one another, it was also a popular place just to hang out.

There was a meandering queue weaving round the store. Finally she reached the front. The woman behind the counter smiled. 'Good morning, how can I help you today?'

'I need to hire a moped. Or at least I think I do. I should probably try one first.'

'Okay. Let me get someone to come and help you.'

As she disappeared out the back, still smiling, Jem heard her phone ping and, pulling it out of her bag, she saw that in response to her photo Holly had sent her a GIF of a coconut falling on someone's head.

Predictably, Ed had left her unread.

Sighing, she looked up just as a man wearing a red baseball cap wandered into the room, clutching a cardboard box. He slid the box onto the counter, glanced up briefly, just long enough for her to catch a flash of green as her eyes bumped into his, and then picked up a clipboard and turned away.

Her pulse twitched, and she felt heat spill over her face. He had clearly seen her, and she waited for him to look up and greet her, noticing in the meantime and almost against her will how his white T-shirt clung to the contoured muscles of his shoulders, but he didn't turn and finally she cleared her throat.

He still didn't turn, and she felt a flicker of irritation. 'Excuse me. Do you think you could help me?'

Now he turned and straightened up, and she felt her pulse jerk forward as eyes the colour of uncut emeralds met hers. Beneath the cap, he was astonishingly, shockingly beautiful. Hard, high cheekbones; a straight jaw and a curving, sensuous mouth that was edged by a dusting of stubble. He might not have noticed her but his looks and height basically commanded attention. 'Help you?' His voice was deep and husky. She liked it.

And she was not the only one, she realised, as the woman standing behind her murmured, 'You sure can, baby.'

A smile tugged at his mouth as his gaze flickered towards the woman, and then he was moving towards Jem with the careless grace of a pirate swaggering across the deck of his ship.

The careless what?

Slightly disconcerted by that mental image, and hoping her face wasn't as hot-looking as it felt, she nodded stiffly. 'Yes, please. If you're not too busy.'

Oh, great. For some reason she couldn't explain, she was using what Holly and Ed called her 'headmistress' voice.

As he came to a stop directly in front of her, her stomach tightened and she felt a prickle beneath her skin like pins and needles.

'How can I be of help?' he said softly.

Her ribs squeezed around her lungs. Up close his eyes were not just green. There were flecks of blue and brown and gold so that it was like looking into a kaleidoscope. And yet there was something raw about him, something irrefutably male that didn't go with those rainbow eyes.

It was impossible to look away.

He knew it too. But then on an island this small he probably had the pick of the women.

'I need some way to get around the island,' she began a little breathlessly, 'so if I could get some advice…'

She felt his narrowed gaze make a slow, assessing sweep of her face.

'From me?' He stared at her for a moment as if he was making a decision. 'Okay, then, let's go out front,' he said finally.

Outside, the smell of oil mingled with the sea air as she followed him to where two lines of mopeds sat on their stands in the sun. Behind them was another line of bicycles. The man stopped and turned to face her and she swallowed hard. She had thought that maybe in daylight he would look more ordinary but if anything the sunlight seemed to accentuate the miraculous lines of his face.

Wishing she still had the buffer of the counter between them, she said quickly, 'So what are my options?'

'You have three. These are the basic ones.' He gestured towards the line of black mopeds. 'They're practical, they do the job, but they're not going to turn heads. Then we have these.' His hand rested lightly on a pistachio-coloured scooter with cream upholstery and a wicker basket. 'They are Italian. A little bit faster, a little bit more stylish.'

'And what's the third? You said there were three.'

Squinting up at the sun, he pulled off his cap and tucked it into his back pocket. 'A good old-fashioned pushbike.' He turned away from the line of mopeds. 'That's probably your best bet. It's what I'd recommend for those of a more cautious disposition.'

She felt anger twitch through her. What did he know about her disposition? 'I don't bet,' she said crisply.

'Exactly. You don't like going outside of your comfort zone.'

Her eyes narrowed. 'Actually I prefer the Italian one.'

'Really?' He seemed amused. 'Ever ridden one before?'

She glared at him. 'No, but my brother has a motorbike.'

'Good for him, but it's you I'm interested in.' His gaze rested on her face and she felt her cheeks grow warm. He meant as a customer, she told herself quickly, but the raw sexual challenge in his green gaze took her breath away.

She watched, panic and anger and something she didn't want to identify fluttering in her throat as he pulled the nearest moped off its stand. 'Then you better give it a test drive but before you do that—' he picked up the helmet that was hooked over the handlebar '—you need to put this on.'

She took the helmet from his hand. Feeling all fingers and thumbs beneath his gaze, she tried to fit it over her head but her bun was too rigid. 'Here, let me—'

Before she could protest, he reached up and heat exploded inside her as his hand grazed her neck and she felt her hair tumble to her shoulders. 'Now try.'

It was a whisper of a touch but as he took a step back she had to force herself to ignore how it had blazed through her, swift and hot like a flame.

This time the helmet went on easily though.

'Right.' He gripped the handlebar. 'This left side is the front brake. The right side is the rear brake and the throttle. Here—' he pointed to some switches '—you have lights, indicator and the horn. Bermudans love their horns.' He gave her the same flicker of a smile as he had to the woman in the store.

'So to start, you turn the key, squeeze the brake, any brake, and then press the ignition. Voila,' he said softly as the engine started. He switched it off. 'Your turn.'

She sat down on the seat and repeated everything he had just shown her.

'Good. Just get used to the throttle. You'll want to keep your feet close to the ground. Now give it a bit of acceleration.'

The moped started to move. Her heart bumped upwards. 'Nice and slow.' His green eyes were watching her intently and the slow burn of his gaze made her skin feel hot and tight. 'Slow and straight. Now see if you can take it round the car park.'

Jem felt a rush of exhilaration as she navigated the parked cars. She could probably run faster than she was moving but being on the moped made her feel like a character in a black and white film. If only Holly were here to see her.

As she came to a stop, she glanced over triumphantly to where the man was standing, but he was gone. Switching off the ignition, she pulled the moped backwards onto its stand, her elation of moments earlier slipping away. But perhaps he'd gone back into the store to do the paperwork, she thought, tugging off the helmet and resting it on the seat.

'Hey there.' She turned, her heart lurching, but a different man was walking towards her, smiling warmly. 'I'm George. How can I help you today?'

'It's okay, someone's already helping me…only I don't know where he went. He was just here…' Her voice faltered as her gaze snagged on a familiar red cap. She frowned. The man was walking along the jetty. 'Where's he going?'

'Who?' George glanced over to where she was looking. 'You mean Chase. Probably out on his boat.'

'You mean he's a fisherman.' Her stomach felt as if it were in free fall. 'But I thought he worked here?'

George shook his head, grinning. 'No, Chase don't work for me.'

Jem stared after the retreating figure, her cheeks burning with shock and confusion.

In the end she put the Italian moped back and rented one of the bicycles. She knew it was ridiculous to let the actions of a stranger, however handsome, affect her decision but Chase's deception had left her feeling off balance and out of depth.

Her throat tightened.

So many people had lied to her already about what they had or hadn't done and what they would do in the future if she'd only give them another chance and she was sick of it. But after Sam's kindness, and with the beach house and the Bermuda sun putting her in a holiday mood, she'd actually started to think that Holly and Ed were right. She could be someone different here. Someone edgy and adventurous and sexy.

Only then Chase Whatever-His-Name-Was had tricked her into thinking he worked at the Cycle Shack. Worse, he had clearly seen her for the sensible, 'put money aside for the bills' kind of woman she was, and after that it was impossible to picture herself riding around on anything other than a pushbike.

But probably it wasn't just that electric, unsettling interaction with Chase that had flattened her mood. It had been a long day. As she let herself into the beach house, her phone pinged and, pulling it out of her bag, she saw that it was a message from her brother.

Skinny dip? Go on, I dare you!

She stared down at the message and then laughed out loud. Except she knew Ed wasn't joking. She glanced at the gently rippling blue sea. He would be the first one in. Nothing ever fazed him. He was up for anything.

Whereas she was always the one who had to do a forfeit. Sometimes her whole life felt like a forfeit.

Raising her arm, she squinted up, then down the beach. It was completely empty as far as the eye could see. Almost as if she were marooned on a desert island.

Go on, I dare you!

Her heart skipped a beat. Could she do it? Could she swim naked in the sea? She had a bikini but Holly had chosen it, which meant that it was so small she might as well not bother wearing it.

So don't? Biting her lip, she glanced up the beach, trembling with excitement. There was nobody around.

Go on, I dare you!

Ignoring the butterflies spiralling up in her stomach, she ran back into the house, tossed her glasses on the table, grabbed a towel from the bathroom, and then quickly, before she could change her mind, she stripped off her clothes and wrapped the towel round her waist.

At the shoreline, she took one last look and then dropped the towel onto the pink sand and waded into the water. It felt lovely, and unlike the sea at home it was completely transparent. I did it, she thought, a pulse of triumph beating across her skin.

What was that?

She froze, her body electric with panic. But probably she was imagining it. Only then she heard it again. Somewhere nearby, someone was whistling. She spun round towards the shore but there was nobody on the beach. Her eyes narrowed on where the bay curved into the sea, and then, heart thumping out of time, she stumbled out of the water. She snatched up her towel and scampered back into the beach house like a startled rabbit, closing the door behind her.

Clutching the towel around her trembling body, she squeezed up against the window frame. But there was nobody there.

And then she saw him, standing upright on a paddle board, drawing the blade through the water with smooth, effortless strokes. Her glasses were still sitting on the table but she didn't need to be wearing them to know who he was. She had only met one person in her life who moved with such careless grace.

She licked her lips. The man she knew only as Chase looked exactly as he had at the harbour.

Except now he was shirtless.

Her breath bottled in her throat. He had looked good in a T-shirt, but there was no superlative that could adequately describe what he looked like without one. Her eyes hovered greedily on his biceps, then locked onto his chest. He was all smooth golden skin and primed muscle. A light scattering of golden hair cut a line into the muscle of his washboard abs, thickening as it disappeared beneath his low-slung board shorts.

She squeezed back into the house. Her mouth was

dry and her skin felt as if it were on fire and beneath her skin, there was chaos. Breathing out unsteadily, she reached up to touch the nape of her neck where she could still feel the imprint of his hand from earlier.

At that exact instant, he looked over at the beach house almost as if he could feel it too and a jolt of electricity crackled down her spine.

But of course he couldn't feel it. Whatever she had imagined at the Cycle Shack had been just that. A figment of her imagination. And for him it had been a game.

He was out of sight now and she slid down against the wall, her cheeks tingling, the sharp tang of shame rising in her throat.

Coming here was a mistake. She wasn't brave enough to be someone else. So even though it would mean breaking her promise, *again*, tomorrow she was going to change her ticket and go back home.

She stayed there for a long time until the sun slipped beneath the horizon and then, still clutching the towel, she climbed into Joan's bed. There was nothing for her here, she thought, gazing through the window at a star-studded night sky. But as her eyes slid shut it seemed as if the stars weren't white, but a dark, glittering green.

CHAPTER TWO

DAMN IT!

Wincing, Chase Farrar held up his hand and stared at the staple he had just embedded into his finger.

He glared accusingly at the stapler. How the hell had that happened? He gave the staple an experimental wiggle but it didn't move. Which meant he would need some tweezers. And he should probably wash it first. It would help loosen it.

Yanking open the door to his office, he stalked down the corridor, nodding at Callum, one of the twenty-member crew of the *Umbra*. There was a medical kit in the sick bay, and at other points dotted around the boat.

He stopped, frowning, a memory of the day before replaying jerkily inside his head.

The medical supplies.

He had left them sitting on the counter at the Cycle Shack. He swore again, this time audibly and with less restraint. He didn't forget things. Back in New York, his PA had once joked that he should be her PA.

'Everything okay, boss?'

Callum had stopped in his tracks, and was staring

at him inquiringly, and briefly he wondered what the crewman would say if he told him the truth. That a pair of grey eyes had thrown him off track and had him pretending to hire out mopeds for a living. But instead he nodded. 'Everything's fine. I just need to get some tweezers.' He held up his hand. 'Speaking of which, I forgot to pick up the medical supplies from town.'

There were other things he'd prefer to have forgotten, like how the woman had raised her chin and not just met his eyes but inspected him, briefly and coolly.

Even before she told him she was on holiday he had known she was a tourist, that much was obvious from her clothes. A teacher, maybe, he thought, hearing the put-down in her husky voice. Although not an experienced one. She was in her mid twenties at most although she was trying her best to look older with those glasses and the way she did her hair.

He made a fist with the hand; the same hand that had brushed against the nape of her neck as he loosened her hair. A pulse of heat danced across his skin in time to the throb in his finger.

Not married either. He could spot 'married' a mile off, with or without a ring. But why did he care either way?

His eyes narrowed.

He didn't.

Forcing himself to focus on the package he had left back at the harbour, he locked eyes with the crewman. 'I need someone to go collect them from the Cycle Shack. Can I leave that with you?'

'Yes, sir.' Callum nodded.

He turned and made his way to the sick bay. He washed his hand, and eased the staple out of his skin with the tweezers. The kit was low on quite a few items and he felt another stab of irritation at his forgetfulness.

This was his boat. The crew was his responsibility, and he took their health and safety seriously. Obviously, accidents happened. He knew that better than anyone but that didn't stop most being avoidable. He was just lucky they were close to shore. Only he didn't like relying on luck.

Snapping the medical kit shut, he hung it back on the wall.

It had been a long time since any woman had got under his skin like that.

For years now, his life had been clearly compartmentalised. In New York, he ran Monmouth Rock, one of the biggest insurance businesses in the world, and when he wasn't working, he worked out and slept. Sometimes he dated. Friends of friends. People in his circle. But he made his intentions—or perhaps a better word would be his limitations—clear right from the start and he never allowed things to get serious.

After everything he'd experienced in his thirty-seven years, casual, short-term, contained was all he could contemplate when it came to relationships. And there was no shortage of women who were happy to play by his rules.

Down here in Bermuda, things were even more clear cut. Instead of work, he used his focus and energy and his immense wealth to look for sunken ships. So all in all, life was good. Simple.

But the blonde at the Cycle Shack had made everything feel a whole lot more complicated.

She had some kind of physical effect on him, made him lose his balance, tangled up his thoughts. He had been so distracted—no, fascinated—by the molten shimmer of her gaze that he had forgotten all about the medical supplies. Truthfully, he would have struggled to remember his own name.

His chest tightened as he remembered how she had blushed when he'd taken off her glasses. Watching the slow flush of pink colour her cheeks, he'd been stunned, enchanted, amazed that there was still someone in the world who would respond like that. And for some reason that had made his libido not just sit up straight but fight to slip its leash.

She had felt it too. He could almost see the tension coming off her frame in waves as she fought against it.

Suddenly needing air, he made his way outside. As he took a few deep breaths, his gaze flickered across the deck to the busy harbour, automatically searching for a glimpse of fluttering blonde hair.

It meant nothing, he thought, turning deliberately to stare at the open sea. She had caught him off guard too, that was all. It was always the same at this time of year.

Maybe he should give Emma a call. She would distract him. Emma was one of the women he hooked up with when he needed a date for an event or to feel skin against skin. She was beautiful and smart and he enjoyed her company in and out of bed. He could fly her down from New York. She would be here in two hours.

Only it was not something he'd ever done before. What if she got the wrong idea?

He frowned. This was her fault. That nameless woman who had somehow managed momentarily to make him forget the past. It was her fault that he needed a distraction.

But it wouldn't happen again. There was no reason for their paths to cross during her holiday so he could forget about that brief flicker of attraction that had passed between them like electricity.

And even if she had been moving here for good, it wouldn't change anything. He wasn't looking for a relationship with someone who still blushed when she talked to a man. Because he wasn't looking for a relationship at all.

Pressing the plunger down on the cafetière, Jem poured herself a cup of coffee and stepped out onto the deck of the beach house.

She had woken late, for her anyway. Holly and Ed were still at that point where they found it a struggle to wake before noon but she had always been a poor sleeper. But last night, lulled by the sound of the waves, she had fallen asleep instantly and woken as sunlight flooded the room.

The same sunlight that was now warming her skin.

She padded down the steps and wriggled her toes in the sand. It was just too perfect, almost as if she were in a film set on a beach. But maybe all holidays felt like this.

Her eyes narrowed into the sunlight. Truthfully she

could barely remember her last holiday. Or perhaps it was another of those things she wanted to forget. She glanced back at the turquoise-coloured ocean. Either way, this was the real deal. Her toes twitched against the pale pink sand. Why, then, was she thinking of leaving?

Not just thinking. Her bag was zipped up, ready to go. She had packed it this morning after showering, scampering around the tiny house, snatching up books and shoes and sunblock, feeling not like the guest she was, but an imposter.

But why?

Green eyes holding hers steady, captive. *Chase.*

She steadied herself, but her breath kept jerking in her throat as she pictured him standing on the paddle board, his clean profile cutting a line across the crisp blue sky. She hadn't chased him but she had done the next best thing, riding in circles even though the moped she'd been sitting on wasn't his to rent.

And now the memory of that moment was chasing her away.

It crushed her to know that. To be such a coward. To not even be able to count how many other times she had let her fear of failure or of being a disappointment get in the way of living her life. There had been that job in Costa Rica restoring the coral reef. She was shortlisted but, having read up on the charity's founders, she had dropped out of the running. They were clever, important people doing important work and she was struggling to finish her thesis so of course she had to withdraw her application. It was one thing to let yourself down but to let down other people would be unforgivable.

She bit into her lip. She wasn't just scared of letting people down. She was scared of confronting them too. Look at how many confrontations she'd failed to have with Nick over his drinking. Only at the back of her mind, she was always terrified of what the consequences might be.

But if she left now, she would have to break her promise to Holly. *Another promise.* Neither of the twins understood why she felt so compelled to date such damaged men. To them it was just a baffling pattern of behaviour that needed to stop. They didn't know it was a form of atonement, and how could she explain that without telling them what she was atoning for?

How each time she failed to save her current boyfriend there was more to atone for, and so it carried on.

It was almost a year since she'd ended things with Frank and sworn to her sister that she wouldn't get so involved next time. That she would keep things casual. Only then she'd met Nick.

When she found him in bed with that woman, nobody said *I told you so*, except Ed, but she knew how upset both he and Holly were, and this holiday was their treat. Could she really let a complete stranger chase her away from this paradise? Bermuda might be small but the chances of her bumping into Chase again were surely remote.

And Holly was right. This wasn't just about having a holiday, it was about rebooting her life, tearing up the rules. Maybe not play with fire but why not strike a few sparks? For starters, she could take back the bike and swap it for one of those ice-cream-coloured mopeds, and later she would check out what was behind the Green Door.

But first she was going to unpack.

After returning the bike, she rode back to the beach house on the pistachio-coloured moped she had tried out with Chase, the wind whipping at the ends of her hair, feeling uncharacteristically cool and sophisticated.

He wasn't all that. Probably if she met him again he would be underwhelming.

If only she knew where he was she could have ridden past him with her nose in the air but instead she spent the rest of the day on the beach, eating the fruit that Joan had left and swimming, this time wearing her bikini. She had also emailed Joan to ask her where she could go diving.

The diving course had been her last birthday present from her father. She didn't count the cottage. You couldn't include something you got left in a will. But other than a few dives off Cornwall she'd never really had a chance to test her skills in real life. That would be tomorrow's challenge. Tonight she was going to go dancing.

Having washed her hair and left it to dry in the warm air, she pulled on a lightweight cream wrap dress and some tan sandals and, remembering Holly's directive, she put in her contact lenses and then added some make-up.

Joan's mirror was as tiny as everything else so all she could look at were sections of herself. But she was surprised to find that she liked what she saw. She dithered momentarily about whether to walk along the beach but in the end she decided to take the moped.

Had Sam not given her directions, she would never have found the Green Door. There was no sign but the door was green and she could hear the music jumping through the evening air even before she switched off the engine. As she pulled off her helmet, her eyes widened. The pubs at home got crowded but this was like a New Year's Eve party. There were people spilling onto the beach, drinking and laughing under a canopy of lights and flowers, and everyone seemed to be smiling.

Inside, it was difficult to see the bar itself. Finally, she managed to get to the front. There were several people working behind the bar. Three men and one very beautiful woman in a clinging red dress. One of the barmen leaned forward. 'What can I get you, baby?'

'Lime and soda, please?' she said quickly. It was her drink of choice at home. It looked enough like alcohol that she didn't stand out in the pub. Her family and friends knew that she didn't drink but she had discovered that it was easier on nights out to pretend she did than be obviously teetotal.

'You must be Jem.'

She glanced up, startled.

'I'm Aliana.' The beautiful woman behind the bar smiled at her. 'Sam told me you might be dropping in.'

'But how did you know who I was?'

Aliana laughed. 'We don't get many tourists out here. Look, I gotta go back to work, but I'll keep my eye on you. Enjoy the vibe.'

She managed to find a table in the back room, and

to her surprise it was easier than she expected to follow Aliana's advice. Normally on nights out, she was so tense, so on edge; she always felt like the 'grown-up' in the room. But here, she wasn't responsible for anyone. She could just sit and watch. As her eyes moved across the room, the crowds parted and she caught a glimpse of a pool table. A game was in progress. One man was standing at the side, his cue upright in his hand like a staff. But it was the other man, the one bent over the table, who caught her attention.

She couldn't see his face but she could almost feel his concentration.

Although how he could concentrate with so much going on around him was anyone's guess, she thought as he potted the ball with an audible crack.

The final ball, apparently. There was applause and cheering and she found herself smiling but as he straightened up she felt her body still. There was something familiar about that back.

At that moment he turned towards her and she felt her face dissolve in shock. Around her, everyone else in the room seemed to fade away. It was him. The man from the Cycle Shack.

Chase.

What was he doing here? Her heart raced at the sight of him. For a moment she just stared, her glass frozen mid-air. Earlier she had imagined herself on the moped, glancing at him with cool confidence, but now that he was standing in front of her she just wanted to run. But it was too late. As if feeling her scrutiny, he looked over and his gaze collided with hers.

Suddenly she was aware of nothing except the dark, uneven thud of her heart.

And his eyes, clear, green, steady on her face.

Her fingers tightened around the glass as a group of women stumbled in front of him, laughing and clutching at one another, and he disappeared from view, and for a moment she thought she might have imagined him, but then the crowd parted and she saw him again, weaving his way through the crowd towards her.

Leave, she told herself fiercely, but she was rooted to the wooden bench. Her stomach clenched as he stopped in front of the table, that same flickering smile pulling at his mouth.

'Hello again.' He paused and she felt her stomach somersault as his green eyes locked with hers. 'How's the moped? Let me guess, you swapped it for the bike, didn't you?'

'I did swap it for the bike. But then I swapped it back,' she added, giving him a small, challenging smile.

'Is that right?'

She nodded. 'I didn't get very good advice.' Lifting her chin, she cleared her throat. 'Apparently the man who helped me didn't actually work at the Cycle Shack.'

His smile widened and she felt her pulse accelerate. 'I spend enough time there it feels like I do.'

'But you don't.'

'No, I don't,' he agreed.

'Well, don't let me keep you from your game, Mr...?' Lifting her drink, she looked pointedly past his shoulder.

'Just call me Chase.'

'Is that your name?' she replied tartly, although she knew it was. 'Or are you just trying it out for tonight?'

He laughed softly. 'It's definitely mine although when I was a kid I used to wish it wasn't. Having a stand-out name at school seemed to get me into more trouble than my friends.' He shrugged. 'But it's a family name.'

He was trouble, all right, she thought, with or without the name, but it suited him. *Chase.* It was what predators did, she thought, her brain spinning like a top. And this man was an apex predator.

He held out his hand and, caught off guard by this sudden formality, she took it. Like everything else about him, his handshake was confident, masculine, firm. Although his mouth looked as if it would soften to kiss a woman.

Her pulse twitched madly as he released his grip, and she flexed her fingers beneath the table to try and shake off the tingling imprint of his touch.

'And you are…?'

'Jemima,' she said stiffly. 'Jemima Friday.'

'Really?' In the pulsing light, his eyes glittered like emeralds. 'Interesting name for a stranger on an island.'

Her mouth was suddenly dry, her throat too tight. 'And you get one Robinson Crusoe joke, so use it wisely.'

He nodded slowly. 'I'll bear that in mind.' Somebody shouted his name and he glanced over his shoulder but he didn't leave. He just stood there looking at her, his green eyes searching her face as if he was making a decision about something.

'Look, about before, I was out of order at the Cycle Shack. I shouldn't have done what I did and I'm sorry.' His eyes dropped to the empty glass in her hand. 'Why don't you let me buy you a drink, to apologise?'

'You don't need to do that.'

'I'd like to. Please, what are you drinking?'

Her insides tightened as he stared down at her. She had told herself that he wasn't that beautiful. That if she met him again she would be underwhelmed. But she had been wrong. Beneath the soft pulsing lights his face was shockingly, arrestingly beautiful.

And she wasn't the only one to notice. Theoretically it was so crowded in the bar that it should be impossible to pick a face from the crowd but Chase was not just inconspicuous, he seemed to exert a gravitational force over the room, judging by how many women were glancing over at him with surreptitious and not so surreptitious glances.

'It's just lime and soda.'

She half expected him to protest, to insist that she have something more exciting from the list on the chalkboard, but he simply nodded. And it was then, watching his shoulders as he made his way to the bar, that she realised he was making the crowd part, he was responsible for the ebb and flow she had seen earlier.

Her heart thudded against her ribs. This was madness. *It's just a drink,* she heard Holly's voice inside her head. *Just enjoy the vibe.*

More than anything she wanted to watch him walk towards her again, but she knew that seeing him move towards her with that tantalising, casual grace would undo her completely. Instead she forced herself to stare across the room at the photos on the wall. They were different sizes and some were curling at the edges with age but the thing they had in common was that they all seemed to picture grinning men standing beside giant suspended fish.

'Are you interested?'

Her pulse jolted forward as Chase appeared beside her. 'In what?' She stared at him in confusion.

'Fishing.' He was holding two glasses of lime and soda, and as he dropped down onto the chair opposite, he slid hers across the table. 'You know, sport fishing. Wahoos, tuna, marlin. The whole Hemingway schtick. Not that he came to Bermuda. He was out in Bimini and the Keys, but sport fishing is a big part of the tourist industry here too.'

He'd read Hemingway. That was a surprise. But why? Fishermen read books too.

She shook her head. 'No, sorry. Is that what you do on your boat? Take tourists out fishing?'

His mouth ticked up at one corner. 'No, I fish for myself.' His green eyes narrowed and she felt his gaze rake over her again.

'So why have you come to Bermuda, then?'

It was a simple enough question but the answer was anything but. Then again, Chase didn't need to know anything but the basics.

She shrugged. 'I just needed a holiday. And I've wanted to visit Bermuda since we did *The Tempest* at school.'

Really? She winced inwardly, hearing the twins'

groan of despair inside her head. Had she actually said that out loud? But it was true. Ever since that term when she studied the play she'd been fascinated by shipwrecks and Bermuda was the shipwreck capital of the world.

'And now you are,' he said softly.

Her heart thudded. The table suddenly felt too small. Or maybe they were sitting too close. She felt something stir inside her as his eyes met hers. He was a stranger and yet no one had ever looked at her so intently as if they were trying to reach inside her. It felt oddly intimate.

Too intimate.

And far too soon. There was still some of Nick's stuff at the cottage.

He leaned forward. 'So what do you think of the "still vex'd Bermoothes"?' She felt another jolt of surprise. Not many people had read *The Tempest*, let alone could quote from it.

'I think it's beautiful,' she said simply.

'So can I tempt you into trying your hand at fishing?' Chase said. His gaze was lazy and yet intent at the same time, like a cat watching a mousehole.

She felt her face grow warm. She had no doubt that there were any number of things Chase could tempt a woman into doing.

'Maybe another time. What I really want to do is go diving.'

He raised an eyebrow. 'You dive?'

His obvious astonishment made her eyes narrow. 'Yes, I dive. Not snorkel. Dive.' She pulled out her phone. 'Here. That's my PADI certification.'

'Okay, okay.' He held up his hands, laughing. 'My bad. It's just you don't seem like an outdoorsy kind of a girl.'

'That's because I'm not a girl. I'm a woman with a PADI certificate for open water and enriched air. I just haven't done it in a while. I've been busy with work.' Not true. 'Busy with life.' Also not true.

He stared at her for a long moment and she held his gaze, her pulse jackhammering in her throat. How could a look make her feel like this? He hadn't even touched her and yet there was something in his eyes that made her feel naked and exposed. She could feel it moving through her, not playfully or gently, but fiercely like lava.

Without warning, he shifted back in his seat and got to his feet and she felt a sharp nip of disappointment, pain almost. So that was that, then.

'Dance with me.'

His words, somewhere between an order and an invitation, were so direct, so at odds with what she was expecting him to say that she stared at him in shock, her breath fluttering in her throat as he held out his hand again.

Back in England Holly and Ed both danced with a complete lack of self-consciousness that she admired but had never managed to emulate. But this wasn't really dancing, she realised as he led her onto the dance floor and the shifting crowd swallowed them up. There was not enough room to dance. Instead, people were clutching each other, grinding rhythmically, their closely packed bodies radiating sweat and heat.

As Chase turned to face her, he leaned closer and she felt his warm breath against her ear. 'Is this too much for you?'

Her stomach knotted fiercely. He was too much for her. Intoxicating like moonshine, she thought as the lights caught the curve of his cheekbone.

Reaching up, she curled her arms around his neck. 'It's not enough,' she said, and his pupils flared and he moved nearer, his hands gripping her waist, anchoring her to him so that she could feel every detail of his body, feel the heat of his skin, the flex of his fingers. Mouth dry, she stared up at him, feeling the air leave her body. She had danced with other men but she had never looked so closely into their eyes, so intently, so intimately. It was fascinating and terrifying in equal measure and she was suddenly desperate to feel his mouth on hers.

They stayed like that for a long time. Finally, the music started to slow and she felt him draw back. 'Let's get some air.'

Outside, the moon was high and silvery in the sky and the cool air made her head and senses swim. It was Chase who broke the silence. 'I'll get Aliana to call you a taxi to take you back to your hotel.'

That was a good idea. Very sensible, she thought. Except she didn't want to be sensible.

You can be anyone you want.

That was what Holly had said, and for one night only she wanted to be wild and passionate and demanding. She wanted to throw caution to the wind. Only if she left now, if she walked away from this beautiful, sexy stranger, she would be just Jemima. Sensible, sedate, sober. Stuck in a rut of failed relationships.

But she didn't want a relationship with this man, she thought dazedly. She wanted sex. Just sweet, mindless sex. Sex without any ties or burdens, without explanations or any kind of data sharing.

Sex. The word fizzed on her tongue. Sex with Chase. Her heart was hammering in her ears. And why not just sex? Nick might have trampled on her heart but she still had a heartbeat and she wanted it to pound tonight.

She cleared her throat. 'Is that what you want?'

He flexed the fingers of his right hand. For a split second she saw his profile dark against the sky. 'I want what you want.'

'And what do I want?' she said huskily.

His green eyes were almost black in the darkness, and he wasn't smiling. A finger of anticipation and excitement tiptoed down her neck.

'I don't want to put words in your mouth. You have to say it,' he said, the roughness in his voice scraping against her skin. 'You have to make it clear what you want.'

For a moment, neither of them spoke. The music was reverberating through her body. She could feel it low in her belly, joining a different, heavier pulse that was impossible to ignore.

She took a step towards him; in doing so she was saying yes. But it wasn't enough. He was right: she had to say it out loud.

'Okay, then. No questions. No conversation. You don't need to know anything about me and I don't want to know anything about you. All I'm looking for is a one-night stand.' It was what she had promised to do back in England. But she wasn't just doing it for Holly. Now that she was here with this beautiful, sexy stranger, she was doing it for herself. 'I want to get naked with you, now, tonight. Is that clear enough?'

The words sounded so blunt, so explicit. She had never spoken like that to anyone in her life and his slow, hot glance trapped her breath in her throat.

There was a hair's breadth of space between them. Tipping back her chin, he stared into her eyes and then his head dipped, his mouth grazed hers and yet there was something fierce beneath it, something hot and dangerous, something that made her melt on the inside. And then he fitted his lips to hers, kissing her hard, a searing kiss, open-mouthed, urgent; a kiss that stole her breath, robbed her of reason, rendered her helpless as he slid one hand around her waist, the other through her hair, his lips and tongue urgent now, his body a hard press against hers.

She arched against him, her hips meeting his, wanting more, skin tingling, blood pulsing hot and fast.

He made her want so much. She could have been anywhere in the world. Truthfully, she could be out in space, drifting among the stars. As soon as his lips had met hers, she was aware of nothing but his kiss.

Pinpricks of light exploded like sparklers inside her head. His desire was so raw, so unfiltered it knocked her off balance, and yet she wanted it all. She wanted him.

His hand dropped from her hair to her collarbone, fingers slipping beneath the dress to find hot, bare skin, making a shivery, tortuous pleasure spiral up inside her. Lips parting, she moaned against his mouth.

He wrenched his mouth from hers, his hands gripping her elbows as she swayed forward. For a moment, he seemed to hesitate, and something rippled over his face—shock, confusion—as when a breeze lifted the surface of a lake, and then it was gone as quickly as it came.

'Let's get out of here,' he said hoarsely.

'And go where?' she whispered, panic mingling with desire.

'Your place. Or mine.'

Her place? She tried to picture Chase in Joan Santos's tiny house. And then there was the morning. How did that work?

'It's probably easier to go to yours.'

He leaned forward and his mouth covered hers again. His eyes were dark, his expression intense. 'My place it is, then.'

He had a motorbike. Of course, he did, she thought as he buckled up her helmet. Leaning onto his strong back, her arms wrapped around his waist, she felt as if she were floating. Blood was beating in her ears and the air streamed past her, dark and cool like water.

His place turned out to be a boat. She waited as he unlocked the gate to the private jetty, and then he took her hand and helped her on board.

Inside, moonlight was streaming through the windows of his cabin. A book lay on the bed, its cover arching up like the roof on a house, and she felt a pinprick of shame at her earlier prejudice, and then she felt his hand in her hair, lifting it away from her neck, and a wall of need slammed through her as his lips found the pulse beating frantically behind her ear.

Dragging in a breath, she turned to face him and kissed him hungrily, her desire making her confident as she realised that with anonymity came mind-blowing freedom.

This was right. This was what she wanted. He was what she wanted. There were no promises to break; no hopes to dash. There was nothing but need—her need for his hard body inside her. A need she saw reflected in those dazzling green eyes.

She ran her hands over his chest, loving the feel of the hard smooth muscles, awed by the difference between them. She could see the hunger in his eyes, the dark flush on his cheekbones. Excitement surged through her and she tugged his shirt over his head, swallowing hard as she saw his bare chest, and the outline of his erection pressing against the fabric of his shorts.

Her mouth was dry; breath trapped in her throat.

She was so ready to start that she was shaking with desire and, hooking her fingers into the waistband of his shorts, she slid them down over his hips.

He sucked in a breath, muscles tensing and, head spinning, she stared at him in silence.

Oh, my goodness.

He was big and hard…very hard.

'Take your clothes off,' he said softly. 'I want to see you naked.'

It was a command, not a request, and the heat in his voice licked at her skin like flame. With hands that shook slightly she undid the belt of her dress and let it slide from her shoulders. His pupils flared but he didn't look away from her face and she kept her eyes trained on his.

Now she undid her bra and dropped it to the floor.

'Stop,' he said hoarsely, and she stood there, her nipples tightening, breasts aching. For a second he stared at her, breathing unsteadily, eyes glittering in the moonlight, face taut with concentration, saying nothing. Just waiting, the electricity between them tangible.

And then she saw his control snap, and he pulled her into his arms, hands palming the swell of her breasts, grazing her taut, aching nipples as he kissed her deeply, thoroughly. She moved against him, arching into the hard press of his erection.

'Yes,' she whispered into his mouth. 'Yes,' she said again as his hands slid down to cup her bottom.

Lifting her slightly, he backed her onto the bed and knelt in front of her. She shivered all the way through as he slid her panties down her thighs. The air was cool against her skin and she felt so bare and her hand moved instinctively to cover herself but he batted it away, his head dipping between her legs.

A moan of pleasure escaped her lips as she felt the tip of his tongue flick against the swollen bud of her clitoris, sending shock waves through her. She shuddered, arching against him, pressing herself closer, wanting more, wanting to answer the seductive, head-spinning ache.

She took a strangled breath, trying to clear her head, to shake the dizziness away, but she was melting into a pool of need. She had never felt anything like this before.

Her head fell back and she clutched at the sheets, her belly clenching, tight and hot. He was teasing her. The tantalising rhythm of his tongue made her think of his body on hers, and in her, and she let go of the sheets and gripped his shoulders, hips arching, a flickering, sharp current of heat surging through her, flooding her limbs.

She felt him move up the bed and then his mouth was hot and damp against hers as he lowered his hips against her pelvis. The press of his erection took her breath away and a shiver of excitement ran through her.

'I want you.' Her fingers wrapped around him and she opened her legs wider.

He grunted. 'Wait—'

He reached past her and yanked open a drawer by the bed. 'Condom,' he said, tearing open the wrapper and sliding it on. Raising himself up, he rubbed the blunt tip between her thighs, stroking back and forth, and then he pushed into her and began to move, slow at first then faster, teasing her still quivering body back to life.

She squirmed against him, not bothering to hold back the moan climbing in her throat, dazzled by the pressure and size of him, muscles tightening on the inside, trying to grip him as he moved against her, his body driving deeper and harder and harder and deeper and then a fierce white heat exploded and she shuddered helplessly beneath him and she felt him tense, his lips brush hers as he groaned her name against her mouth, jerking forward, hips arching as he thrust inside her.

CHAPTER THREE

BLINKING DROWSILY, Jem fluttered her eyes open. It was the light that had woken her, pressing against her eyelids and pulling her from the darkness of sleep. Light from a pale, soft-edged sun, although she had fallen asleep with moonlight streaming through the same window.

She glanced round the boat, body stiffening as her brain tried to make sense of its surroundings, and then she remembered everything. The impossible pressure of Chase's body on her, and how she had shaken with need and eagerness as his hands, his tongue unravelled her into a shuddering, breathless frenzy.

Her face felt warm.

All was calm now.

And she didn't need to remember the impossible pressure of Chase's body because he was there beside her, his arm heavy across her waist. He was still sleeping, his chest and stomach curved around her back, his unshaven cheek nestling against her shoulder.

Chase what?

Her breath caught as she realised that she didn't even know his surname. But then why did she need to know it? She wasn't taking a register. For what she wanted, she didn't need to know his full name.

And it wasn't just his name she didn't know. There were no words to explain how he had made her feel last night. But it was enough to have done this; to know how his body felt on hers and inside her. To have stretched out beneath his glittering, green gaze, stripped not just of clothes but all inhibition and restraint, with his pulse beating through her.

She felt her body ripple to life and for a fraction of a second she considered rolling over and reaching for him as they had done over and over again in the moonlight, but if she did that then he would wake up and then what?

Her heart began beating a little faster. She had no idea what the etiquette was for the morning after the night before. Should she stay and say goodbye? Was that what people did?

Maybe.

Or maybe there were different rules on holiday. Surely most people got up and left because, like her, they weren't looking for conversation and commitment. She stared out of the window at the steadily rising sun. After all, wasn't that the point of a one-night stand? There was no second act. No finding your true love. Like the fairy godmother's spell, the magic wore off, if not at midnight then soon after. Footmen became mice again. And in this case, a lover would simply turn back into a handsome stranger with whom she had nothing in common except a desire for one passionate encounter.

Her chest was suddenly tight around her heart. In the story, not all the magic wore off: true love triumphed and Cinderella found her happy ever after. But that was just a story, she thought, glancing round the neat but shabby cabin. And Chase was a fisherman, not a prince. As for happy ever afters, maybe they did exist outside fairy tales; for other people, maybe, just not for her.

The sharp cry of a bird outside brought her back to the here and now and she felt a sudden rush of panic. Shifting noiselessly onto her side, she gazed over at the man beside her.

Chase was still asleep, one arm thrown across the pillow, his face in shadow, but there wasn't much time. It was seven-fifteen according to the old-fashioned alarm clock on the bedside table, but in another few minutes the sun would creep across those movie-star features and then he would be rubbing his face and sitting up, his hair ruffled, his green eyes half open and soft.

Her breath caught in her throat, and suddenly she was fighting the wild beating of her heart. He really was a fantasy come to life, and what they had shared had felt like a fantasy too because it was. What made it so intensely erotic was the fact that there was no need for any jarring return to reality. No morning after. No uncomfortable sharing of space. No awkward conversation.

Reaching out, she brushed a strand of hair away from his forehead.

He'd been so generous and she'd felt so alive, so free, so completely without inhibition. She didn't want to ruin the memory of all that by letting reality intrude.

So there's your answer, she told herself. *It's time to leave.*

It was harder than she thought to extract herself from

Chase's arm, to abandon the delicious warmth of his body. She dressed, holding her breath, her heart beating in her mouth as Chase shifted in his sleep. Picking up her sandals, she tiptoed to the door, then turned back to the bed.

She was never going to see him again. And yet she would never forget him either. But then she knew that right from the start. She hesitated, torn between panic and her need to be polite. There was an envelope on the bedside table and a pen. She hesitated again, then began writing. Leaning forward, she rested the note on the bedside table and then she turned and crept back out of the cabin and into the pale dawn light.

'Excuse me, boss.'

Chase swung round, his forehead creasing. 'What is it?'

His first officer, Alex, was standing at his elbow. 'We just got an update on that depression. It looks like it's getting bigger, and it's going to come pretty close.'

'So?' He frowned, his eyes narrowing with poorly concealed irritation. 'We've had closer and bigger storms.'

'Yes, sir.' Alex paused. 'Thank you, sir.'

He felt rather than saw Alex retreat. Behind his back, he could sense the other crew members on the bridge catching each other's eyes and that only added to an irritation he knew was both unfair and disproportionate.

But then he had been tetchy since he stepped foot on the bridge. Not because of the storm. Storms he could handle. What had made him so testy was waking this morning to find his bed empty even though Jemima Friday should never have been in his bed in the first place. Mouth twisting, he replayed the events of the night before. He shouldn't have gone over to talk to her at the Green Door. That was his first mistake. No, his second, he corrected himself. His first was pretending he worked at the Cycle Shack.

He scowled down at the electronic charting display screen, his jaw tightening. So many mistakes, all equally out of character. He didn't sleep with women he met in bars. And the one and only time he'd had one-night stands was right at the very beginning after Frida's death when his grief and guilt were so agonising that it hurt to breathe. He couldn't have coped with affection or intimacy then. He had simply wanted oblivion and the easiest way to achieve that goal was to self-medicate with alcohol. Lots of it. And, to wash it all down, meaningless sex with strangers.

Outside the window, a gull was soaring through the sky. He had read somewhere that a gull's wing was about as near as nature got to perfection. Hard to disagree with that, he thought as he watched it drift effortlessly on the thermals, noting the more rounded shape of its silver-grey wings. Wings that were almost the same colour as Jemima's eyes.

The gull wheeled away, and he stared at the empty sky.

There had been nothing meaningless about sex with Jemima. On the contrary, even now, hours after he was inside her body, his own body was still twitching with the memory of their fever dream of a sexual encounter.

And hard and aching for a round two that wasn't going to happen.

Only apparently the memo from his brain detailing the one-night status of last night had gone missing en route to his groin.

His fingers twitched against the screen. What the hell had he been thinking? He hadn't needed to approach her at the bar. He could have ignored her.

Should have ignored her and he definitely should never have asked her to dance. And when they went outside, he should have got Aliana to call a cab and sent her back to her hotel. But he hadn't done any of those things.

Instead, he had taken her back to the boat. Not the *Miranda*. At least he hadn't lost his mind completely. For some reason, Jemima thought he was a fisherman and he had seen no reason to disabuse her of that fact, so he'd taken her to the boat he kept down by the shoreline.

He had bought the boat as a favour. It was not worth fixing but he liked to spend a few hours whenever he was on the island just tinkering with it. Or sometimes he would stay up and fish on those nights when he couldn't sleep.

The tension in his body spilled over his shoulders. He hadn't slept much last night. Waking, he had almost thought he had dreamt what happened but then he'd seen the note. It took every ounce of willpower he had not to reach into the pocket of his shorts and pull it out. Not that he needed to. He could remember every word.

Thanks for a wonderful night. Tight lines. J.

Tight lines. He chewed on the words angrily.

He knew the phrase. It was something a fisherman might say to a mate instead of wishing him good luck.

His lip curled as he remembered her insistence that last night be a one-night-only thing. Coupled with her unannounced and unexpectedly precipitous departure this morning, it was clear that Jemima Friday had friend-zoned him. And he didn't know why it should be getting under his skin, but every time he replayed those words inside his head a fresh surge of fury would rise up inside him.

When even was the last time a woman had given him the brush off? He was more accustomed to his dates trying to make what amounted to friends with benefits into something more serious.

Not Jemima.

And much as he disliked admitting it, that annoyed him. She had been so eager and responsive last night. Then again, when they had first met at the Cycle Shack he'd had her down as the shy, sensible type. Only how did that square with the woman he'd met at the Green Door who said she wanted to get naked with him? Heart accelerating, he wondered which Jemima was the real one.

He felt a tic of irritation pulse across his skin.

The only correct answer to that question was who cared? And yet, frustratingly, he found that he did care.

And what made it doubly baffling and frustrating was that she had made him remember how good sex was.

Obviously he'd had sex. It had been eight years since

the accident and he wasn't a monk. But after Frida, sex had been simply an itch to scratch. It was pleasurable, for both parties, but not personal. And yet somehow this woman, this stranger, had changed that, made him want her.

Probably because she had upped and left like Cinderella running from the ball. Only instead of leaving a shoe, she had left that note. Now he reached into his pocket, and he felt his temper stir again as his fingers brushed against it. He knew that if he had woken to find Jemima still in his bed, he would have been desperate to get rid of her. That was how it worked. In the cold light of day, the magic of the previous night faded abruptly. Everything lost its sparkle.

But when he woke she wasn't still in his bed. At some point between when he had pulled her against his drowsy body and the sun rousing him from sleep, she had sneaked out on him, which meant there had been no jolt back to reality.

So now she was stuck in his head, her naked body bathed in moonlight, skin gleaming with perspiration, blonde hair spilling over her shoulders.

His phone vibrated in his other pocket and, grateful for the distraction, he retrieved it and pressed his thumb against the sensor. Reading the text, he felt some of the tension ease from his shoulders. Marcus was not the most eloquent of communicators but at least some things were happening the way they were supposed to. All he needed to do was concentrate on those and soon enough Jemima Friday would turn into Jemima Last Week.

* * *

Stepping out of the boutique, Jem slid her sunglasses on and glanced cautiously down the street. But there was no sign of any broad-shouldered man in a red cap.

She hadn't planned to come into Hamilton.

After leaving Chase's boat, she had made her way to the road and had been on the verge of calling Sam to pick her up when a bus arrived. To her astonishment, the driver had been willing to drop her off some two hundred metres from the Green Door. Perhaps it was his unhesitating and cheerful flexibility or maybe it was the infusion of post-orgasm endorphins in her body but, having collected her moped, instead of returning to the beach house she had found herself heading towards the capital.

She glanced down at the glossy rope-handled bag dangling from her hand. She hadn't planned on buying the dress either.

Clothes shopping was something she did under duress. Holly was the shopaholic in the family, but then she had been walking past one of the boutiques on Front Street and she had seen it in the window.

It was not something she would buy ordinarily. For starters it was yellow. And it was short, too boho, and definitely too expensive, but the Jem who had woken that morning was looking for something to match her mood. Something casual and confident. And buying a beautiful dress on a whim was exactly what casual, confident Jem would do.

Feeling unshakeable, she'd walked straight into the shop and asked to try it on and everything had been going fine until it was time to pay and she had started chatting to the woman running the store.

'So how long are you staying in Bermy?'

'Just another week.' She'd smiled. 'Are you a local?'

The woman had nodded. 'Lived here all my life.'

'Any tips for a first-time visitor?'

She had many. Don't buy fruit from the last stall in the marketplace. Church Bay was the best spot for snorkelling. And the best breakfast in town was at Bocado.

'I mean saltfish and banana, not bacon and egg. But you need to jet down there now before the men get back off the boats.'

She had smiled again and thanked the woman but, at the mention of men getting 'back off the boats', casual, confident Jem had melted away like ice cream in direct sunlight.

Feeling nervous and breathless, she walked quickly across the square to where her moped was sitting on its stand. With hands that trembled slightly she packed her shopping into the wicker flower basket. There was no real reason to panic, she told herself. Although Hamilton was not big, the chances of her running into Chase Whatever-His-Name-Was in town had to be slim at best.

But even the possibility of it made her whole body feel taut and achy and restless, as if she had ants under her skin.

By the time she reached the turn-off that led to the beach house some of her panic had subsided and she was calm enough to slow down as she went round the corners. Not that it was necessary. Since arriving she hadn't seen cars.

Her eyes widened with surprise. There were not one, but two pick-ups parked on the edge of the track, the kind driven by builders. She stared at them uncertainly. There were no other houses on this stretch of beach. Maybe they were working further up the beach. But as she approached the house, she saw the door was open and through it she could hear the sound of vigorous hammering. Stepping inside, she almost dropped her bags.

The kitchen was in disarray. The fridge was standing forlornly on the deck next to the old sink. A new sink, still shrink-wrapped in bluish plastic, sat next to it like the before and after shot in a fashion magazine.

'What do you think you're doing?'

The men turned towards her in unison. The surprise and confusion on their faces were not reassuring. Still clutching her bags, she took a step closer. 'Who are you, and what are you doing in my house?'

The man standing nearest cleared his throat. 'We work for Mr Farrar, ma'am. We're here to do the refurbishment.' He gave her a mollifying smile. 'It's all arranged.'

She shook her head. 'Not with me, it wasn't.'

Reaching into his back pocket, the same man pulled out his phone and scrolled down the screen. 'It's all here. Kitchen and bathroom refurbishment, starting today.'

Bathroom.

She swung round, mouth dropping as she stared into the bathroom or what was left of it. Everything was gone. The sink. The toilet. The shower. All that remained were some pipes sticking forlornly out of the wall.

Breathing shakily, she leaned against the doorframe to steady herself. How was this happening? Not just happening, it had already happened, she thought, her eyes darting around the devastated bathroom again. 'How long will it take to make it good again?'

The man rubbed his hand across his jaw. 'About a week. It's not just the fixtures. A lot of the pipes need replacing.'

'A week.' Jem stared at him in horror. 'And what am I supposed to do?' Her gaze swung back to the bathroom, panic swamping her. She couldn't stay here without a toilet or running water, but she didn't have the money to stay in a hotel or a B & B.

'No, that isn't going to work for me. Look, you're going to have to put it back,' she said firmly.

'Put it back?'

As three men stood and stared at her with a mixture of disbelief and bemusement, the last of her endorphins drained away and she felt suddenly exhausted and exasperated. This was her holiday. She hadn't asked to have the beach house refurbished so why was it suddenly her problem to solve?

'Yes, put it back,' she repeated.

One of the other men shook his head. 'Boss ain't going to like this,' he muttered.

'I don't care what your boss likes or doesn't like,' she said stiffly. 'He is irrelevant.'

'I'm not sure that's either fair or true but I've been called worse.' A deep, oddly familiar voice resonated around the tiny house and they all turned as one towards its owner.

A man was standing in the doorway, sunlight framing his muscular body as if he were some celestial deity come to earth to intervene in mortal matters. *No*, not just a man, Jem thought, shock pounding through her in a clattering drum roll. It was Chase.

She suddenly couldn't breathe. But what was he doing here? She watched dazedly as he shook hands with each of the men before turning towards her. 'Chase Farrar,' he said, his green eyes flicking to her face as if he'd heard her question even though she hadn't asked it. 'I'm the irrelevant boss and your proxy landlord.'

Her heart was banging like a gong. *Farrar.* She'd heard that name before. Her brain lit up like a fruit machine hitting the jackpot. This was Farrar's Cove. But surely it was just a coincidence.

'I don't understand,' she said slowly. 'What does that mean?'

'It means what it says. I'm the landlord, so, as you can see, I am perhaps a little more relevant than you thought.'

There was a slight edge to his voice. But why? He wasn't the one who had come back to find his house being ripped apart by strangers.

She gestured towards the wreckage of the bathroom. 'I can't live like this—'

'Of course not,' he cut her off smoothly. 'But as far as I was aware Ms Santos had made arrangements to stay somewhere else while the work was being done. I only found out she had someone staying here when

I emailed her this morning to confirm the schedule of work and she said you were doing a house swap with her.' His eyes locked with hers and her heart thudded hard and she felt something stir inside her, her body betraying her. 'I thought I'd better come over and see how things were going.'

'Well, I don't have a bathroom or a kitchen so I would say they were going badly.' Her voice sounded shrill and she knew that it was revealing more than she wanted about how she was feeling, but she couldn't seem to do anything about it.

She felt a prickle of frustration. It was bad enough that her holiday home was now a building site, but that she had to be dealing with the one man on the island she most wanted to avoid seemed just too unfair, not to say unbelievable, to be true.

And yet here he was.

'I would have to agree with you.'

Chase was staring down at her, his green eyes steady on her face, that mouth of his flickering at one corner. And just like that she remembered how he had kissed her, remembered the feel of his lips on her and the rough urgency of his hands.

Her pulse leaped in her veins and, terrified that he might be able to read her mind, she batted away the memory and lifted her chin. 'Good, then it seems like we're all in agreement.'

The man who had spoken to her before cleared his throat. 'The lady wants us to put it all back, boss.'

She watched as Chase turned towards him and smiled. 'Thanks, Marcus, but I think I can take it from here. Why don't you and the guys take an early lunch while I sort things out with Ms Friday?'

He phrased it as a question, as if it were optional, but there was no mistaking the commanding note in his voice. What had possessed her to think that this man was a simple fisherman? Jem thought as the men shuffled out of the door. As she stood here in the shell of the beach-house kitchen it felt utterly obvious that Chase Farrar was not simply a fisherman. It wasn't just his manner. Now that she looked more closely, she could tell that his boat shoes were not the kind you picked up at the local sailing outfitters. Only she had ignored the signs because that was what she always did.

Like with Nick.

She knew that, beneath his charm and good looks, he was flaky and weak and damaged. But she didn't date regular men who got paid and remembered your birthday and told you the truth about where they'd been.

And in the same way she had sensed that Chase was more than he appeared to be. To anyone else—her sister, for example—that would be a red flag, but she couldn't help herself. The louder the alarm bells, the more she wanted to stay and make things right.

And yet she still felt played. Stupid. Small. Just hours ago it had felt as if she had unlocked a different side of herself with this man. And it had all seemed so real, but just like at the harbour he had been pretending to be someone he wasn't. Her arms tightened around the bags she was holding. Their night together wasn't a moment of truth. It was all a hoax, and now she felt like a fraud.

But she wasn't about to tell Chase that. She had already shared too much of herself with this man. She wasn't going to let him have anything else.

'Sort things out? And how exactly are you going to do that?' she said sharply. 'Or are you a plumber as well as everything else?'

She was using that voice again, Chase thought, his eyes resting on Jemima's face. The one that reminded him of the principal at his high school. Few, if any, people spoke to him in that way. It was one of the consequences of being a high-net-worth individual: people tended to fawn over him. They certainly didn't use that dismissive tone or look at him as if he were some stray dog who had followed them home.

'I can put you up in a hotel for however long it takes. You don't believe me?' he said coolly as her lip curled.

'The first time we met you pretended to be working at the Cycle Shack, and last night you let me think you were a fisherman, so forgive me if I'm not inclined to believe anything you say.'

Reaching out, he took the bags from her arms and dumped them on what remained of the kitchen counter. 'I fish.'

Her eyes flashed, the grey swallowing up her pupils. 'But you're not a fisherman.'

'And you're not staying in a hotel,' he countered.

Her face stilled. 'I didn't say I was.'

'No, but you let me think you were.'

'That's different.'

He heard the catch in her voice. It was. But it also wasn't.

'Was that even your boat?' she said quietly after a moment of silence.

He frowned. 'Of course it was.'

'There's no "of course" about it.' She glanced past him, her lip trembling. 'You know what, don't worry about it. I don't need your help. I can sort things out myself. And you, you can go back to living your "lives".' And before he had a chance to open his mouth, she had turned and stalked out of the door.

Staring after her, he felt a ripple of irritation. He wasn't to blame for any of this. In fact, if she'd told him where she was staying he would have been able to postpone the work—again—and then none of this would be happening.

But it was, and somehow he was tangled up in it, tangled up with her.

His heart beat jarringly inside his chest. This wasn't who he was. When it came to dealing with women he never crossed any lines, but Jemima and Joan had made it so that the lines were not just blurred but overlapping. He gritted his teeth. He wasn't responsible.

Or perhaps, in a way, he was. He had seen Jemima in the bar but he could have left her alone. But he hadn't, and one thing had led to another and he'd kissed her. And he could have, should have left it at that, only then she'd kissed him back and he'd been derailed, hot and horny as a teenage boy.

He found her down by the shoreline. She wasn't crying but she was close. He could tell by the set of her shoulders and the way she was staring fixedly out to sea, her phone clutched in her hand. And he didn't like how that made him feel.

But then he didn't like feeling anything at all. For him, feelings, caring for someone, about someone, were in the past. Aside from the most impersonal version of lust, those feelings, like certain kinds of caresses, were something that were off the menu when it came to his interactions with women. He'd shut that part of himself down; he'd had to. He didn't have it in him to take on someone else in that way. Only there was something about Jemima, a wariness in those beautiful grey eyes that he understood. As if she was expecting the ceiling to crack apart and fall on her head. Because it had already done so.

He knew that feeling well.

'Who are you calling?' he said gruffly.

'A hotel. They don't have any rooms.' She breathed out shakily. 'She said that it will be really difficult to find a room because of the boat parade.'

He swore silently. Of course. He'd forgotten it was this weekend. There would be twenty thousand extra visitors on the island.

'So what are you going to do, then?'

She glanced up at him. "I'm going to do what I should have done in the first place. I'm going to go to the airport and change my ticket and get the first flight back home that I can.'

He frowned. She was leaving?

'You don't need to do that.'

She was shaking her head. 'I knew it was a mistake coming here. This isn't who I am. I should have never let them talk me into it.'

'Hey...' Reaching out, he caught her shoulders and turned her to face him. 'Slow down. Who talked you into what?'

Her lips quivered. 'My brother and sister. They booked this holiday for me as a treat and now it's all ruined.'

The gentlest of breezes was catching her hair and lifting it away from her face and as he studied her profile he felt himself responding, just as he had at the harbour and then again at the bar. He gritted his teeth. But he didn't have to sort this out personally. He had people on the island who could deal with it. He had people all around the globe to deal with the slightest hiccup in his life, and yet...

'It's not ruined, and you shouldn't go back home. You'll regret it if you do and there's no reason for you to do so.'

She sniffed. 'That's easy for you to say. You're not living on a building site.'

'And you won't be either. Look, this is just one of those things that happen sometimes. But it's my builders who ripped a hole in your beach house and your holiday.'

He hesitated. 'So let me help you.'

'Help me how?'

'I have a house here. Not on the main island, on one of the smaller ones.' She stared up at him, her eyes wide with shock and confusion as if she couldn't believe what he was saying, and that made two of them because he couldn't quite believe it either. But now that he had said it, he felt a complete and total conviction that it was the only option.

'I know what you're thinking but you don't need to worry about me being there. I'm taking the boat out tonight and I won't be back for a good few days, so you can stay there until the work is done.'

Her belly clenched as he stared down into her pale, wary face. 'Unless that's going to cause a problem with your boyfriend.'

'I don't have a boyfriend.' She glanced past him to where the waves were rolling against the sand. 'I don't do relationships.'

He stared at her profile, saying nothing, wondering why that statement both pleased and agitated him. 'I don't do them either so go and get your bag packed because you're coming with me,' he said finally. 'And I'm not taking no for an answer.'

CHAPTER FOUR

Dusk was falling.

Eyes narrowing, Jemima gazed across the water. It wasn't just the sky that was darkening, the sea was now the colour of new denim except where a dark orange line bled into the horizon.

The speedboat was hugging the coastline of the island, which she had since learned was not an island at all but an archipelago made up of around one hundred and twenty islands. The main island itself was actually eight smaller islands linked by bridges.

But then in her experience things were so rarely what they seemed. Situations, actions and people could all confuse and deceive.

Her pulse darted forward in time to the slap of the waves against the hull. Take Chase Farrar, for example. He was a man who fished but most definitely wasn't a fisherman. And yet this was his glossy, high-spec speedboat that was scudding across the waves with smooth, expensive purpose. His hands were calloused and rough like a working man's but he had that backbeat of authority in his voice that made people stand up straighter and listen.

And apparently he owned an island. Her gaze fixed on the fast-approaching curve of pink sand that was just about visible in the fading light. This island: Bowen's Cay.

Her throat tightened. He had told her that as she got into the speedboat and she still couldn't quite believe it. But maybe land was cheaper out here.

Flashes of panic at the prospect of staying in Chase's house made her skin shiver. Although given that he wasn't going to be staying, this was probably the riskiest part of their time together. Which was why she was keeping her gaze firmly averted from the man driving the speedboat.

Unfortunately she didn't need to see Chase to be aware of him. She was unnecessarily attuned to his every move. Sometimes she got so distracted she forgot to breathe.

A light offshore breeze was whipping through her hair and she was grateful for the additional oxygen as she wondered, not for the first time, if she'd made the right decision agreeing to stay in his home.

Should she have kept trying to find alternative accommodation? Maybe. But she could tell from the receptionist's voice that she was highly unlikely to find a room at such short notice. She could have listened to her gut and seen it as a sign that she wasn't meant to be here at all. And a part of her had really wanted to scuttle back to England to the safety of her own, tiny cottage.

Only then she had looked up into his eyes and remembered how she had scuttled back into the beach house when he'd interrupted her skinny dip and she'd felt ashamed of herself, of her fear and her timidity.

And in that moment she had known that if she went back to England she would always be that timid, fearful person.

Besides, going back to England would mean having to see Holly's disappointed face and Ed's despairing one. In comparison, Chase's offer seemed like a blissfully straightforward solution to her problem, a problem that was at least some of his making. After all, it was his men who had turned her idyllic holiday home into a building site.

Her heart thumped against her ribs. This wasn't some Faustian pact. And it would only be for a week at most and it wasn't as if he were even going to be there.

She felt the boat slow and glanced up, her throat tightening as Chase switched off the engine. A tall man wearing Bermuda shorts and a polo shirt stepped forward and deftly caught the prow of the boat. A slim, dark-haired woman in similar clothes stood beside him, smiling.

'Good evening, Mr Farrar. Welcome home.'

She watched Chase step onto the jetty with the same casual grace with which he did everything and then nearly jumped out of her skin as his hand clamped around her elbow. 'Here, let me help you.'

He was just being polite, she told herself, but as he released his grip, she took a quick step sideways, her hands curling into fists to stop herself from rubbing the place where his fingers touched her skin.

'This is Ms Friday. She'll be staying at the house. Jemima, this is Robyn and Troy. They will be looking after you.'

'A pleasure to meet you, Ms Friday.' Troy smiled. 'I hope you enjoy your stay.'

'Thank you.'

Troy glanced up at the sky.

'It's going to be a close thing tonight, boss.'

Chase nodded. 'I reckon so.'

'The house is just up here.' As they walked along the path it lit up ahead of them like a landing strip. Which was both impressive and lucky, she thought, glancing up at the sky. It must be cloudy because there were no stars tonight. It made the sky feel closer somehow, the sea too.

She shivered, the butterflies back in her stomach again, and then quite suddenly the house appeared out of the lush tropical vegetation. It was, she decided, more a hideaway than a house. A piece of treasure plucked from the seabed cupped in a hand.

There were a couple of steps leading up to a wide wooden veranda and Jemima followed him cautiously inside. 'I'll give you a quick tour of the house,' he said, turning to give her one of those blink-and-you-miss-it smiles.

He wasn't kidding, she thought as Chase walked swiftly through the house, opening doors and rattling off the names of the rooms. There was an urgency to the tour, as if he had somewhere he'd rather be, which he did, she reminded herself. But it was the coolness of his manner that was getting under her skin.

Irritated by the sheer stupidity of that thought, she turned her attention to the house.

Here, unlike on the main island, there were no pastels, no eye-popping candy colour. Instead, the decor was understated and masculine, a luxurious mix of wooden floors, pale walls and architectural-looking furniture. The lighting was soft and unobtrusive like a harvest moon.

'And this will be your room,' he said abruptly as she followed him upstairs and through yet another door.

'It's lovely,' she said, because it was. Her eyes moved appreciatively from the curved rattan bed with its white voile curtains to a vase of delicate pale green orchids.

'There's a dressing room through there.' He indicated another door. 'For when you want to unpack.'

She glanced back over to where her bags were sitting neatly by the bed.

The bed.

It had been turned down, one corner of the duvet folded back invitingly to reveal a smooth white sheet, and her cheeks grew warm as she remembered the tangle of sheets on the bed on Chase's boat and the contours of his body as they melted into one another.

She could feel his level gaze raking her face, and, needing to get away from him and the bed, she turned towards a second door and said quickly, 'What's in here?'

It was the bathroom. A very beautiful bathroom with a free-standing marble bath and a walk-in shower that could happily fit a football team. There was a selection of toiletries in matt, metallic tins and she picked one up, her eyes widening as she read the list of ingredients. White clay. *Camu-camu*—whatever that was. Orange flower water. Vetiver and passion-fruit oils.

'It's there to be used, so help yourself to anything you want.'

Her chin jerked upwards, and she blinked. Chase was standing behind her, his gaze resting on her reflection. In this light, the irises were the colour of the pine forests at home and she felt a mix of hunger and homesickness so intense that her belly clenched painfully.

'Thank you.' Dropping her gaze, she put the tin down carefully as if it were a newly laid egg. He was so close she could feel the warmth of his body, and the scent of his skin, his scent, enveloped her. As she breathed it in, her eyes met his reflection again and she felt fingers of heat low in her belly, impossible to ignore.

He was doing this to her, she thought, fighting panic. He was making her feel all hot and confused and on edge. But how? They barely knew each other. And yet with him, she felt she knew herself better. Which was crazy and utterly illogical.

'Are you hungry?' he asked, breaking the taut silence.

Yes: but not for food.

The knots inside her tightened. It was a small consolation that she hadn't said it out loud but something in his eyes made her think that he had heard her unspoken thoughts.

She shook her head. 'No, I'm actually quite tired. It's been a long day. I might call it a night.'

Night.

The word whispered between them, conjuring up darkness and the white heat of his skin in the moonlight, and for a moment neither of them spoke, and then he nodded. 'Good idea. I need to speak to Robyn and then I'll be heading back to the boat. Enjoy the rest of your holiday. I'll get someone to let you know when you can get back into the beach house.' He hesitated, a muscle flickering in his jaw, and she felt a tremor ripple through her as his green gaze roamed her face.

'Get some sleep, Jemima,' he said softly, and then he turned and strode back the way they had come.

Was that it?

She stared around the empty bathroom feeling oddly disappointed by his sudden departure. Which was ridiculous as she'd not even said goodbye to him this morning.

Her heartbeat stalled against her ribs. Was it only this morning? It felt like a lifetime ago. No wonder she was feeling so thrown. But it wasn't just the timescale that was messing with her head. Less than twenty-four hours ago they had been tearing each other's clothes off in a frenzy of passion and need. Now he was talking to her as if she were a guest at his hotel. The distance between them was putting her teeth on edge.

In the bathroom, she glanced at the bath, then the shower. But she could wait until tomorrow. For some reason she felt oddly shy about getting undressed when Chase was in the house, which was also ridiculous given that he had already seen her naked. And not just seen her. He had touched her too.

She screwed up her face, irritated to find Chase Farrar back in her head again. He wasn't supposed to be there but, probably because she was in his house, every thought she had seemed to lead inexorably to him.

But only if you let it, she told herself crossly. She brushed her teeth without looking in the mirror and then forced herself to undress slowly. Pulling on an oversized T-shirt, she climbed into bed.

It was like climbing onto a cloud. Or what she imagined it might feel like climbing onto a cloud. Soft and cocooning yet also inexplicably light. And yet she couldn't fall asleep.

Shifting onto her side, she shivered all the way through. She knew why. Being here in Chase's house was obviously going to be unsettling. But if she wasn't going to let him back into bed with her, she was damned if she was going to let him back into her head. It must be the waves keeping her awake, she told herself firmly. She could hear them through the window and they sounded louder than last night, heavier almost. But perhaps this particular island was more exposed.

She must have fallen asleep at some point because she woke with a jolt, her heart hammering against her ribs. Rolling over, she found her phone and clicked on the screen. It was not even ten o'clock. She lay there in the darkness for a few moments, but this had happened so many times in the past she knew there was no point in just lying there.

It was better to get up and get a cup of camomile tea and read a book than watch the clock mark the hour and half-hour until dawn. And if Robyn wasn't up, she could easily sort herself out.

The house itself was silent but the sound of the wind and the waves accompanied her as she made her way downstairs. She was using the torch on her phone to guide her but everything felt different in the darkness and the sound of her feet moving lightly across the smooth floorboards made her feel like an intruder, not a guest.

Wishing she could switch on the lights, she tiptoed into the living room only to realise that it wasn't necessary. Eyes widening, she stopped to gaze through the huge floor-to-ceiling windows that covered three sides of the room.

There was a storm out at sea. High above the white-capped waves the lightning was criss-crossing the night sky, flickering between the dark, scudding clouds like a strobe light at a rock concert.

'Impressive, isn't it?'

The voice caught her by surprise, and, startled, she spun round. Her stomach did a tiny, clumsy somersault. Chase was sprawled out on the sofa, his green eyes gleaming catlike in the shadows, a laptop half open on the coffee table beside him.

'It's amazing,' she agreed, pressing her hand against a nearby armchair to steady herself. What was he doing up? Why did he have to be here now?

His gaze skimmed lightly across her oversized T-shirt, and her body reacted, the hair on her arms prickling to attention, her breasts suddenly heavy against the light cotton fabric. He had changed clothes too. Now he was wearing grey sweatpants and a black T-shirt, and his hair looked tousled as if he'd been sleeping. Actually he looked like an invitation to sin, she thought, her heart jumping in her throat as he sat up and stretched, his T-shirt tightening around his contoured chest.

But just because she'd played with fire and not got burnt, didn't mean that she should stir the embers, and, hoping that none of what she was thinking was visible on her face, she said, 'I thought you were going back to your boat.'

He shrugged. 'Storm came in bigger and closer and faster than predicted so I decided to wait until morning and catch up on my emails instead.' He gestured towards the laptop. 'That's the great thing about the modern world: someone's always at work somewhere.'

His green eyes found hers and, needing distance from that too intense gaze, she took a step backwards. 'I'm sorry, I didn't mean to disturb you.'

Chase stared at Jemima in silence, his whole body tensing.

It was a bit late for that, he thought. The storm might have stopped him from getting back to the *Miranda*, but Jemima was the reason he was wide awake, lying on this sofa, pretending to read his emails. Apparently knowing that she was lying in bed in the same house as him was a green light for his imagination so that his head was full to bursting with feverish images of her.

And that was before she'd come tiptoeing into the living room wearing nothing but a T-shirt. It was shapeless and so oversized that it would be impossible to guess at what lay beneath. Unfortunately, he didn't need to guess.

'You didn't.'

Although she had. 'I was just watching the fireworks.' He gestured towards where lightning was still forking through the clouds accompanied by a distant growl of thunder. 'Did they wake you?'

She shook her head. 'I don't think so. I think it's just being in another different bed.' There was a short silence as her eyes juddered across the space between them to meet his, then flicked away, and he noticed a blush creeping up her neck and into her cheeks.

And just like before, he found that he couldn't look away.

He cleared his throat.

'No, it's fine,' she said quickly. 'I just thought I might make myself a cup of herbal tea but it's really not that important.'

'Help yourself. The kitchen's through there.'

Leaning forward, Chase reached for his laptop. 'Or I could just show you,' he said, shutting it firmly even though he had definitely been intending to check the weather forecasts again when he'd picked it up.

And yet here he was standing up and walking into the kitchen because he wasn't sure if she would take him up on his offer and then she would leave, and he didn't think he wanted that. Although it was difficult to know why he wanted her to stay, but, truthfully, wanting someone, wanting her, was such a rarity for him at this point in his life that he was as fascinated by it as he had been by that blush.

In the kitchen, he dumped his laptop on the counter and switched on the lights. 'Take a seat,' he said, directing her to the stools nestling around the breakfast bar, and stared assessingly at the bank of pale oak cupboards.

'What would you like?' He pulled open a cupboard, stared at the contents and then tried another. Then another, and another.

'Do you want me to help?'

'No…actually, yes, I have no idea where anything is,' he admitted, opening another cupboard and staring at the jars of various kinds of rice. 'Mostly Robyn fixes things for me.'

He caught a flash of grey as her eyes clashed momentarily with his and then she leaned forward to open one of the drawers and he forgot all about her eyes as the hem of her T-shirt hitched up to reveal the backs of her thighs.

His body stilled.

It was all too easy to remember those same thighs wrapped around his hips in the moonlight as she lifted her body to meet his. That night that had ended too soon, only now she was here. In his house. In that T-shirt that wasn't designed to arouse in any way. And yet…

He clenched his hands tight, then tighter still so that he had something to focus on other than the ache in his groin, and, back in control, he turned and yanked open another drawer. Thank goodness! 'Here we go.' He stared down with relief at the carefully organised rows of tea. 'We have peppermint, ginger and turmeric, camomile, lavender and valerian root. I'm going to keep going until you pick one.'

She cleared her throat. 'Camomile would be lovely.'

During the time it took to fill the teapot with boiling water, she watched him while appearing not to, in the same way that an antelope would watch a dozing leopard.

'Are you not having one?' she said as he put the teapot on the breakfast bar and handed her a cup and saucer.

He shook his head. 'I'm not a fan. But I might grab something to eat. Why don't you join me?' Without asking, he picked up the teapot and filled her cup. He didn't know if she wanted to drink it now but it was something to do while he waited for his brain to offer up an explanation as to why that was a good idea.

It was just politeness, he reassured himself. But his invitation echoed inside his head just like at the beach when he had asked her, in a roundabout way, if she had a boyfriend.

He couldn't remember the last time he'd blushed but he felt his skin grow warm now. Jemima's life back in England was none of his business and yet, inexplicably, he had wanted to be sure she was single.

She was shaking her head. 'I'm not hungry.' But as she spoke, her stomach gave an audible rumble and she bit into her lip, and as their eyes met he felt a rush of triumph as she tried and failed to stop her mouth curving at the corners.

'Well, maybe I am a little bit,' she conceded.

'You're in luck,' he said, opening the huge larder fridge. 'This is one of Robyn's specialities.'

'What is it?' She looked down at the bowl he had put in front of her.

'It's a *poke* bowl.'

Watching the flicker of curiosity in her grey eyes reminded him of the clear waters of Lake Superior where he grew up. Of fishing with his father and cook-outs with his cousins. Back then he had been a different person. Back then he hadn't known what the world had in store for him. He was young and naive. He didn't know how quickly things could end or how badly. He didn't know then that there was a pain that could drag you down and leave you gasping for breath beyond the reach of the sun.

His chest tightened. Over time, the scars had healed, hardened and now he didn't have to worry about feeling pain. He didn't have to worry about feeling anything. Nothing except basic needs. Thirst. Hunger. Desire. But they could all be contained.

'Robyn comes from Hawaii. *Poke* is practically the national dish out there. Basically it's meat and fish and vegetables and fruit chopped up into tiny pieces. That's what *poke* means in Hawaiian—to chop up.'

She stared down at the neatly chopped rainbow arrangement of rice, beetroot, edamame and avocado. 'It's so pretty.'

'And delicious.' He held out a fork. 'Here, eat.' She did, and he watched with some amusement as she sampled each of the various components.

'Good?'

She nodded. 'The flavours are incredible.'

They were. And he'd thought he was hungry, but

weirdly he found that his appetite seemed to have disappeared, so that it was a struggle to even lift the fork to his mouth.

'So do you come from Hawaii too?'

He glanced across the table, momentarily caught off guard, not so much by her actual question but by her sudden trespass into the personal. Most of the women he knew didn't ask him much about himself. But then most of the women knew all they needed to know.

'No, I come from Minnesota, from a small town near Lake Superior. And you?'

She hesitated. 'A village in the Peak District.'

Shifting back on the stool, he held her gaze. 'We have something in common,' he said softly. 'Except I left and you stayed.'

Now she frowned. 'I didn't come from Edale. I was born in Sweden, and then I lived in Ireland. I didn't move to England until I was four.'

'Why Sweden?'

She shrugged. 'My mother is Swedish.'

That explained the colour of her hair. As his gaze touched her head, he remembered how the silken strands had felt in his hands.

'And what about your dad?'

'English.'

She didn't blush this time, but she glanced away as if she didn't want him to see her eyes and he knew that she was hiding something. Holding something back. He couldn't see the barricades she'd raised between them, but he could sense them. So that was another thing they had in common.

He watched her chew on her lip. He shouldn't care, and yet he found himself wanting to prise her apart like an oyster.

'You didn't say what you do back in England, job-wise I mean,' he said at last. But then the last time they met, neither of them had been interested in small talk. There was a silence as both of them separately acknowledged that fact.

She cleared her throat. 'It didn't come up.'

He met her gaze. 'No, I suppose it didn't,' he said softly.

A faint flush suffused her cheeks. For a few seconds, she didn't reply and then finally she put down her fork. 'I don't really have a job. I help out in the university bookshop and sometimes I do a bit of tutoring but I'm actually working on my PhD.' She looked up at him almost defiantly as if he might challenge her. 'It's on "accidental" reefs.'

The phrase was familiar but not in any detail. 'And what does that mean, exactly?' He was interested.

Jemima hesitated. 'I suppose in layman's terms it's when a wreck becomes a reef. Basically from the moment a vessel sinks the ocean takes over. It starts to form a new underwater habitat. Over time, fish colonise the wreck. Algae and corals grow on the surface and the currents draw in clouds of plankton, which attract fish, which in turn entice sharks and other larger predators. Eels and groupers move into the darker spaces. The wreck creates a whole new ecosystem.'

He stared over at her, captivated by the light in her eyes. 'Why "accidental reefs"?'

'I did a degree and a masters in ecology, and one of my lecturers had a lot of bottom time. He got me interested but it was my sister who badgered me into doing the PhD.' She gave him a small, careful smile. 'She's a force of nature. My brother is too.'

It was a habit of hers, he'd noticed, to introduce her siblings into the conversation when things got too personal and he found himself wondering why she used them as a shield.

'I thought the general consensus was that wrecks are a menace, even some of the older ones.'

He was interested enough in the topic but it was Jemima herself who was holding his attention. She listened, an unusual enough quality in itself. But she was also assessing and evaluating what he said, whereas most people tended to value only their own viewpoint. No wonder she was doing a PhD.

'There's been a lot of research done on the negative impacts,' she admitted. 'You know, pollution from leaking fuel and rust particles. But wrecks exist. It's important to find a way to live with the negative.'

'Don't make perfect the enemy of the good,' he said softly.

Another blush. 'Exactly. You can't change the past, you have to improve on it. That's why I'm interested in the positives.'

'Which are?'

Watching her forehead crease, he found himself fighting the urge to reach over and smooth her forehead with his thumb.

'For starters, it protects the natural reefs from divers, particularly where tourism relies on diving trips.'

He nodded, and as he did so he realised something. He had been tense for weeks. It was always like that in the run-up to the anniversary of his wife's death. His body seemed to clench in on itself. He lost his appetite and his nights were interrupted with tangled, febrile dreams, but, listening to Jemima talk, he felt as if she had laid a cool hand against his forehead.

'And in the future as ocean temperatures rise, artificial reefs can help certain marine species migrate towards more suitable habitats nearer the poles. Anyway—' she cleared her throat '—that's enough about me, what about you? What's your job?'

His eyes held hers. 'Is that how this works? You show me yours and I'll show you mine?'

A drop of pink spread slowly across her cheekbones. 'It seems only fair.'

Fair. Shifting in his chair, he felt his throat tighten. That she still wanted, expected things to be fair made him feel suddenly protective of her. And grateful that she had never experienced the loss and loneliness and grief that he had.

'I'm in insurance. Reinsurance, mostly.'

'Is that a joke?' She stared at him, her grey eyes narrowing in disbelief.

'No. I set up my own business about ten years ago.' Holding her gaze, he smiled. 'Although I do know some pretty good insurance jokes if you're interested. The one involving an actuary and the magic lamp is my favourite.'

'Maybe another time.' She gave him another of those measured stares. 'So your boat is just for leisure?'

He felt his ego protest at that assessment. 'Not leisure, sweetheart,' he said, shaking his head. 'Treasure.'

'Treasure?' she echoed softly, and, watching her lips soften around the word, he had a near ungovernable desire to lean forward and taste her surprise.

'When I want to relax I come down to Bermuda and look for treasure.' Turning round, he reached for his laptop. 'I start by looking for shipwrecks. That's why I have a house here.'

It wasn't quite as simple as that.

After the accident, he had wanted to stay down in the void that was his pain. It had felt as if there were nothing else. His parents, his friends had all tried to help him with his grief, but he hadn't wanted their help. He had wanted to be alone. It was what he deserved and so he had hired a boat from Beaufort in North Carolina and taken it out in bad weather that got worse. Got dangerous.

He had grown up on the shores of the biggest lake in North America. Sailing was not just a hobby, it was part of everyday life, like cereal for breakfast, so that he couldn't remember ever learning how to sail. It was just something he did, like walking. And he was a good sailor, but that day was the closest he ever came to losing control of a boat.

He spent two days wrestling with the sea, barely sleeping, raging at the wind and the waves. On the morning of the third day, the storm blew out. Checking his phone, he read through the increasingly panicky texts from what looked like his entire contacts list. And in that moment of exhaustion and reprieve, he realised that he couldn't just give up. That he had no choice but to keep moving forward. That if he gave up then he would pass the baton of misery on to them.

As the sun had risen and flooded the sky with a thin golden light he had seen Bermuda for the first time, and he had felt a kind of kinship with the island. Like him, it weathered the storms of life, and like Bermuda he would have to be separate and alone.

It had to be that way. He wouldn't, he couldn't do it again. He couldn't care, feel, need…

Opposite him, Jemima tucked a strand of hair behind her ear and he remembered its glossy weight and how it had suggested all manner of possibilities to him.

Impossibilities, he told himself firmly, flipping open his laptop.

'Because Bermuda has more shipwrecks per square mile than any other place on the planet,' she said slowly.

He nodded. 'That's what they say.'

'And you look for them.'

Tapping the keyboard, he nodded. 'That's exactly what I do. Whenever I can, I come down to Bermy and go looking for wrecks. Like this one.'

She glanced at the screen, her eyes widening.

'That was our last big find. It's a Spanish boat, from a convoy that sank in October 1715.' He clicked through the photos, talking her through the artefacts, but instead of looking at the screen, he found himself watching Jemima's face. She listened with her whole body, he thought, and, gazing down at the curve of her breasts, he felt his own body harden, and for a few pulsing seconds he considered pushing the laptop off the breakfast bar and lifting her onto it and seeing what happened.

'Doesn't it damage the wreck?'

She was looking straight into his eyes, and, caught off balance between the eager, responsive woman in his head and the reality frowning up at him, he was harsher than he intended to be. 'It's a wreck, Jemima. The clue's in the name.'

'Yes, but there's a whole community of marine life there.' She pointed at the screen and the disappointment in her voice snagged on his skin. Most women purred with excitement when they found out he looked for treasure, but Jemima was making him feel like a jerk.

'And we work around it. Look, I've done it all. Base jumping. Free climbing. White-water rafting. This is the biggest rush.'

'So that's all it is for you? An adrenaline rush.'

Watching her mouth flatten, he felt the starkness of her words stick in his throat as he shrugged. 'Adrenaline is good for you. It can block pain. Help you breathe. Improve your sight, boost your immune system.' Intensify your pleasure, he thought silently as she stared up at him.

'But there's so much more to it than that,' she said quietly.

For the second time in as many less than five minutes, his ego rebelled against her dismissive tone. He could have told her that he employed a team of marine archaeologists, and that Farrar Exploration was committed to displaying the finds in museums. He could have told that, after years of working punishing hours to build a global business worth billions, he had earned the right to take three months off every year to comb the ocean for its secrets. But why should he have to defend himself to some snarky little student eco-warrior? This wasn't some college debate.

'More than what?'

'Short-term pleasure.'

'There's nothing wrong with short-term pleasure,' he said softly.

He watched, waited and, sure enough, her cheeks turned pink.

'I didn't say there was,' she said stiffly. 'I just don't think that the ocean is there to be plundered for thrills.'

'Thrills make money. And money makes the world go round.'

'You're very cynical.'

'And you're very naive.'

'I'm not naive.' Outrage shone out of her eyes. 'I just think it would be so much better if we all concentrated our efforts on something other than satisfying our own transitory, selfish agendas. Because the world is doing its best to sustain us, but it needs our help.'

Her face was flushed and she looked a little stunned by her outburst, and he felt ashamed suddenly of how jaded he must seem and he might have even told her so if she hadn't suddenly slid off the stool. 'Thank you for the food. I'll be sure to tell Robyn how delicious it was. I'll let you get back to your emails.'

'I'll see you at breakfast.' He got to his feet too and suddenly they were both standing, and close enough that he could see her pulse beating in her throat. For a moment, they stared at one another, and then she blinked.

'I don't really eat breakfast.'

'That's a shame. Robyn does the most fantastic croissants.'

He thought for a moment that she was going to tell him where to put his croissants, but instead, she said, 'Goodnight,' in that absurdly stiff principal's voice and stalked out of the kitchen.

The sudden silence in the empty kitchen made his shoulders tighten and he put his hand over his heart, feeling it beating out of time. Watching her face light up with that flare of passion reminded him of how she had caught fire in his arms. She might have left that morning, but he hadn't been able to forget that night, and now he pictured her mouth, pink and swollen from his kisses, her blonde hair tangled against the pillow.

The air twitched around him. In that moment they had felt so close, so connected, but that was the trick sex played on people. Away from the unravelling heat of the bedroom, he and Jemima were not just different, they were poles apart. She thought the world was benign and that you could work with it to make things better, whereas he knew that life was dangerous and cruel and random, and you had to be constantly vigilant to counteract that threat.

In other words, he and Jemima had nothing to offer one another except on one level. But he could resist her. After what he'd been through, he had no doubt of that.

The trouble was he wasn't sure he wanted to.

CHAPTER FIVE

OPENING HER EYES, Jemima stared confusedly around the darkened bedroom. But then it wasn't that surprising to feel a little disoriented given that she was waking in her third different bed in as many nights.

And she hadn't slept well mainly because despite having said goodnight to Chase Farrar in the kitchen, he had stayed stubbornly inside her head. Only in her head, she had kept her cool instead of blushing and getting all worked up.

She bit into her lip. She never should have said anything. It was none of her business what he did or why he did it. But watching his eyes narrow on some unseen prize at the bottom of the ocean had made her realise that the only difference between Chase and all the other men she'd ever dated was that, rather than needing alcohol or gambling, he was a thrill-seeker, a man addicted to the adrenaline rush of diving for treasure.

In other words, instead of breaking the bad habits of the past as she'd promised, she was simply repeating them.

That was why she had reacted as she had. It was a

shock hearing him talk in that way because she had thought he was different from all the other men she had fallen for. But it turned out that she had simply proved her sister's theory that she was only attracted to sexy but ultimately unreliable addicts.

Feeling a rush of exasperation with both the old and the new Jemima, she rolled out of bed and padded into the bathroom. What she needed was a shower and, peeling off her T-shirt, she stepped under the water, turning the temperature up until it was punchingly hot.

Closing her eyes, she tipped back her head so that the water ran down her back, turning slowly on the spot. It felt good. Fight fire with fire, she told herself as the heat pierced her skin. And that was what she needed to do now: fight this crazy pull of attraction she felt for Chase.

Her skin was tingling now and she switched off the water and wrapped herself in a cloud-soft white towel, and then, bending over, she wrapped another towel around her wet hair to form a turban. Straightening, she stared at her reflection in the mirror, her pulse shivering as she remembered his green eyes, that flicker of heat.

She had felt it again last night in the kitchen. Low in her belly, impossible to ignore.

Her fingers trembled against the towel. It was crazy to feel like this about someone she hardly knew. What was even crazier was how close she had come to kissing him again last night. She looked at her reflection again, depressed by the colour in her cheeks and the glitter in her eyes. But there was no point in pretending. She had wanted him.

Wanted to touch him and be touched. Wanted his hands to slide over her body.

And then what?

She stared at her reflection angrily. Did she really want to have sex with Chase Farrar again?

Her body felt suddenly hot and tight. Yes, she thought, remembering the friction of his skin against hers. A thousand times yes. But things were already way more complicated than they were supposed to be. And it didn't matter that his touch had melted her with its heat. In fact that by itself was a reason to keep her distance. Chase was a fantasy. Or rather the man who had ordered her to strip naked, the man who made her body feel like a living work of art, was a fantasy. The reality was that he was as addicted to 'thrills' as Nick was to alcohol.

Not that it mattered because she was done with men like him. Done with obsessing about how to decipher their complicated, conflicted lives.

It was better that he stayed as a beautiful memory, she told herself. Only it was difficult when she was living under his roof, sharing a meal with him.

Walking back into the bedroom, she opened the curtains. Her eyes widened. The sky was the warm gold of a ripe peach. The storm had gone. And soon Chase would be gone too. All she had to do was stay strong until then.

There was nobody in the kitchen but she could smell the warm scent of freshly cooked pastry. Outside, she found the source of the smell. A plate of croissants, steam spiralling up from their crisp golden outer shells.

Beside them sat another plate of beautifully sliced fresh fruit and a bowl of what looked like Bircher muesli. But it wasn't just the food that looked so appetising. The table was set with a creaseless white tablecloth and fine, white china.

It looked nothing like her own table at home with its circular stains from Ed's coffee mugs and all her mismatched crockery. Fantasy versus reality, she thought, walking away from the table to the Perspex balustrade that edged the deck, her eyes leapfrogging across the curve of pink sand to the shimmering turquoise water.

Slipping off her glasses, she rubbed them against the hem of her blouse but there was no sign of last night's storm. If she hadn't seen it with her own eyes she might have thought that it was just a dream. Only a slight ripple on the surface of the ocean.

What the...?

She blinked as Chase emerged from the waves, rearing up like some kind of mythical sea god, his blond hair slicked back against his skull. He had his back to her and she stared at the water trickling down his shoulders, her heart pounding inside her chest.

It was one thing having dinner in her T-shirt... It was another to eat breakfast sitting opposite that. She took an unsteady step backwards.

There was an audible crash as her leg collided with the table, the sound snapping around the quiet cove like a gunshot, and she froze as Chase's chin jerked up and he spun round to face her. He'd said he was in insurance, she thought, her mouth drying as his eyes locked onto her with the precision of a sniper. She couldn't imagine why he would lie about that, and to be fair she hadn't met that many insurance brokers, but it was hard to imagine any of them looking like the man standing in the sea like a temptingly masculine riposte to Botticelli's *The Birth of Venus*.

For a moment they just stared at one another and then he started to wade back through the water with slow, strong strides.

But not slow enough, she thought as he came to a stop in front of her moments later. 'Good morning,' he said softly. 'I didn't know you were up.'

'Good morning.' She gave him a small, tight smile, keeping her gaze firmly locked on his face as he pulled a T-shirt over his head. 'I think breakfast is ready,' she said unnecessarily as he could see the table too. But there was something about this man that made her say stupid, unnecessary things.

And made her act on impulses she didn't even know she had.

It was easier once they were both seated and he was no longer shirtless to eat and talk. Their conversation was insubstantial, partly because Robyn appeared at intervals to replenish her coffee and clear away their plates, but also because after last night it seemed wiser to stick to banalities. It also gave her a chance to admire the house.

The design was less colonial than the typical Bermudian house. Instead it seemed to take its cue from one of those hill towns in Italy. The large deck where they were sitting acted as a kind of piazza, with the living area housed in an adjacent bungalow. Two separate bungalows perched above it, angled away from one another to create privacy and provide access to views.

'What are your plans for today?'

Chase's voice pulled her back into the moment and she turned, smiling stiffly. 'I don't know. I haven't really thought about it but don't let me keep you.'

There was a beat of silence and he leaned back in his chair, his eyes narrowing against the sunlight. 'I'm taking the boats out into open water. The ocean opens up its secrets after a big storm so it's a good time to go hunting.'

She nodded. 'So I've heard.'

When she was about four years old her parents had moved to the west of Ireland. After a storm, people used to go down to the beach at Streedagh to look for gold because rumour had it that when the Spanish Armada retreated, some of the boats got separated from the fleet and they ended up being smashed on the rocks off the coast there.

They hadn't lived there long. The lure of the pub had caused the rows between her parents to become even more frequent and explosive and they had moved back to England after just a few months.

Chase was watching her idly but something in his gaze made her feel like a bird with a cat's paw on its tail. 'Why hear it from other people? Come and see for yourself.'

'What? Go with you, you mean? No, I don't think that's a good idea,' she protested. More time with Chase? After what had so nearly happened last night? No. Definitely not.

'Why not? It's just a regular day trip but without all the hassle.'

Why not?

She stared at him in silence, a roaring noise in her ears as she replayed that moment in the kitchen when they stood staring at one another with the tension between them pulled to snapping point.

He leaned forward and she suddenly got a glimpse of that authority she'd seen at the beach house. 'You said you wanted to dive.'

'I do.'

'But what? You'd rather be doing easy duck dives with a bunch of clueless tourists?'

She felt her temper flare. 'I didn't say that. But I don't have any equipment.'

'But I do. Come on, Jemima.' His use of her name made her stomach flip over. 'You want to dive, so let's go take a look at your "reefs".'

The glitter in his green eyes made her want to reach out and touch his face and some of her anger dissipated. It would be madness to agree but, then again, surely there was no real risk of anything happening with the two of them wearing wetsuits and fins.

'Okay, then,' she said slowly.

'Great.' Pushing back his chair, he got to his feet.

'What are you doing?'

He grinned then, one of those slow, curling smiles that wrapped around her throat so that it was difficult to catch her breath. 'Going fishing! Come on.' And as he pulled her to her feet she felt a sudden rush of excitement just as if she were standing like a surfer on the shifting edge of a wave, her body quivering with tension and anticipation.

* * *

In less than ten minutes, Chase had chivvied her out of the house with an even more streamlined set of belongings and into a dune buggy and then they were bumping across a track towards what he called the dock. She was expecting some kind of basic jetty but as they turned a corner her mouth dropped open.

There were not one but six jetties and everything looked custom-made. That thought was confirmed a moment later when Chase said, 'We only finished the construction work on the floating decks two months ago. They're state of the art, designed to handle a storm surge of ten feet.'

She nodded but she wasn't looking at the jetties. Her eyes were fixed on the boats moored beside them on the turquoise water, in particular the largest one, a stunning white yacht, actually make that a superyacht, she thought, breath catching, as her eyes travelled the length of the boat from the stern to the bow. 'That's the *Miranda*,' Chase said softly as he slowed the buggy to a stop and switched off the engine.

She felt her pulse miss a beat. 'After *The Tempest*?'

He nodded. 'Seemed appropriate.'

Their eyes met and she felt a flutter of happiness rise up inside her. Then feeling suddenly exposed, she glanced back to the gleaming white yacht.

'She's beautiful.'

'I think so.' He seemed pleased. 'And that one is the *Umbra*. She's the support vessel, the workhorse. Not as pretty but her beauty lies in her functionality. That's where we keep the dive store and all the tools—

you know, the DPVs, the submersibles, the amphibious
plane. Oh, and there are some of the usual toys for just
letting off steam: jet skis, hydrofoil boards.'

The submersibles? An amphibious plane?

The words were still echoing inside her head as they
made their way through the yacht. She smiled politely as
various crew members were introduced. Her head was
bursting with all this new information, and most, if not
all of it, seemed to contradict her first impression of the
man she'd met at the harbour. A man she had thought
was just some local fisherman who now turned out to
be the owner of a fleet of boats as well as an island.

How had she got Chase so wrong?

*Because he led you to believe he was something he
wasn't.* Her shoulders bowed a little as Holly's voice
popped into her head.

And you didn't ask him the right questions, Ed
chimed in. *You never do because if you did, you couldn't
in all conscience date most of the idiots you end up with.*

That's not fair, she countered angrily. *You were the
ones telling me to let my hair down. So I did, I had a
one-night stand. Surely the point of casual sex is that
it's casual. You don't need or want to know anything.*

And she hadn't: not even his surname.

Exactly. She could practically see Holly rolling her
eyes. *And nothing's changed. He's still a one-night
stand. He just happens to be a one-night stand who
owns an island and a yacht.*

And an amphibious plane, Ed added. *Which is awe-
some, by the way, but doesn't alter the fact that you're
on holiday and this is about having fun, remember?*

I am having fun, she protested.

But Holly and Ed had disappeared, probably in disgust that she had travelled thousands of miles simply to miss the point.

'You can use this room.' Chase swung open a door. 'I'll get someone to bring you a wetsuit and you can get changed.' Stepping into the cabin, she nodded mutely. The decor was similar to the interior of the house. There was rattan furniture, pale walls and eau-de-nil furnishings and all of it hinted at a scale of wealth where money was no object.

'Is everything okay?'

Chase's voice, cool and deep like the ocean, made her turn round. 'Yes.' She nodded. 'But what was the name of your insurance company again?'

He hadn't told her, and she knew from the tiny pause before he answered that he was trying to work something out in his head before he did. 'Monmouth Rock,' he said at last.

She stared at him, her heart jumping in her throat. She knew next to nothing about insurance, but there couldn't be many people on the planet who didn't know that name. She could even picture the logo: the towering dark rock rising out of the foam-topped waves. It was on the front of that football shirt she had bought for her brother's birthday.

'You own Monmouth Rock.'

It was a statement, not a question, but he nodded anyway.

'I'm the majority shareholder.' His green eyes were opaque, impossible to read. Gazing up at him, she felt the jumble of pieces inside her head that hadn't seemed to fit together suddenly slotting together to make a picture. Chase Farrar was one of the super-rich, those mythical creatures for whom ordinary problems like paying the mortgage were mere pinpricks.

And what about pleasure?

Her skin felt suddenly hot and tight. If you could do anything, go anywhere; if nothing was beyond your reach then no doubt ordinary pleasures would seem just that. Ordinary. Dull. Uninspiring.

No wonder he was here chasing treasure.

'I see.'

His shoulders shifted. 'It didn't seem important when we met.' He meant important enough to share with someone he was simply having sex with. And he was right, she thought, mentally listing the many things she could have told Chase, but had chosen not to, for exactly the same reason.

'I suppose not.'

He stared at her for a few seconds, his green gaze burning into hers, and she held her breath, aware that they were alone, and terrified suddenly that he would want something in return. A kiss, a secret.

You show me yours… I show you mine…

'Come up on deck when you're ready,' he said curtly and then he turned and stalked out of the room, closing the door behind him.

As promised, one of the crew members brought her a wetsuit, and she stripped down to her bikini. The wetsuit fitted like a glove, as it should, and she felt another flicker of excitement as she made her way to the deck.

Five people were already suited up, including Chase. As he walked towards her with that familiar lazy, dangerous ease she felt her stomach quiver. That five-millimetre neoprene was hugging his body in all the right places.

'It's a good fit,' he said, his gaze moving critically over her in a way that made the wetsuit feel as if it were dissolving into her skin.

'Okay then, time to swap onto the dive boat.'

'We're diving here?' She had expected them to go further out to sea.

'That's the thing about Bermy. You only have to go a couple of hundred metres from shore and it gets deep real quick. That's why it's so popular with divers.'

The dive boat was a lot smaller than the *Miranda*, but it was still spacious enough for six divers and two other crew members to stand in a semicircle around Chase.

'So, there's going to be six of us diving.' His gaze moved slowly round the semicircle. 'Billy, Dale, Jonah, Linda, me and Ms Friday, who will be joining us today. Ms Friday is doing research for her PhD.' The crew either smiled or raised their hand in acknowledgement and then their gazes snapped back to Chase and she wondered again why she had ever thought this man hired out cycles and mopeds for a living.

'We should be able to fit in three separate dives today. Dive site is eighty feet down. Water visibility is coming in just under two hundred feet so bottles on and then we'll do a buddy check.'

A buddy check was a standard procedure on every dive she had ever done. Basically it was a pre-dive safety checklist. And a buddy, well, it was exactly what it sounded like. A diving partner who kept an eye on you under the water.

Jemima swallowed. 'Who's my buddy?' She said it quickly to get it out of the way, but she knew what his answer was going to be even before he answered.

'I am, of course. We're probably not quite matched in experience but we have a connection.'

Her heart lurched and a trickle of excitement that had nothing to do with the dive wove through her, picking up speed as it travelled as his eyes rested on her face, green and steady and unblinking.

'Don't worry, I know it's been a while, but I'll be right beside you,' he said softly.

They ran through the checks and she was surprised and relieved at how much she remembered. Finally, the last check was complete.

The sunlight on the water was dazzling.

She felt Chase's hand on her shoulder. As she turned to face him, he gave her the thumbs up, and she returned the gesture and then they both took a giant stride away from the boat.

How could she have left it so long? That was her first thought as she entered the water.

It was like jumping into another world. Or into a living work of art. A pristine watercolour as mesmerising as any Monet only down here the colour was not static like on a canvas. It was constantly changing, darkening or growing brighter, shifting in the rippling forks of sunlight.

That she had forgotten.

Chase was right, she thought, with a pulse of excite-

ment. The visibility was incredible. It was like looking through glass. Around her technicolour fish were
darting jerkily in every direction, apparently unfazed
by the gleaming grey sharks and rays that moved la-
zily through them in overlapping ellipses. And there,
covered in shivering sponges and lurid pink and orange
coral that looked too garish to be real, lay the wreck.

Turning, she tapped Chase on the arm and he nodded
and they swam down lower. The boat was on its side.
Some parts had disintegrated but the shape of the hull
was clearly visible and fish were flitting in and out of
the shadowy interior.

She swam towards a pair of angelfish, then got distracted by a bright yellow trumpet fish moving verti-
cally through the water. And all the time Chase was
there, keeping pace with her.

Within what felt like no time at all, it was time to
surface.

Back on the boat, she was elated.

'That was amazing,' she said, pulling off her mask
and blinking into the sunlight. She turned to Chase and,
without thinking, she grabbed his hands and squeezed
them with excitement. 'I've seen footage on the Internet
but that was so much more incredible than I could have
imagined. There were so many species.' She knew she
was babbling but she couldn't stop the spate of words.
'Imagine if more people knew about this.' Her smile
faded. 'Oh, but I forgot to take any photos.'

'It's fine, we've got another two dives, remember?
These guys are going to move on after lunch.' He jerked

his head towards the other divers. 'But I can take you down this afternoon.'

His words made her blink and, suddenly aware of the press of his fingers, she let go of his hands. 'I thought this was your dive site.'

Shaking his head, he gave her one of those quick, devastating smiles. 'We don't dive until we have a reason to, and so far I haven't had a reason. As for this site, locals stripped this wreck bare years ago. I just thought it would be good for your research.'

Her pulse was jerking against the skin of her throat. 'You did that for me?' she said slowly.

He frowned. 'You sound surprised.'

Probably because she was, but why? Okay, Chase was cocky and hedonistic and he wanted different things in life from her, but he was letting her stay in his house, and taking her diving. And in bed he had been more than considerate. He had been generous, fierce, tender, using his hands, his mouth, his tongue, his body to unravel and transform her.

She felt his gaze on the side of her face, and, blanking her mind to that memory, she shook her head. 'I suppose I am a little. After what you said yesterday evening, I thought you'd want to get on with your treasure hunt.'

Her pulse thudded at her temples as his eyes rested on her face. 'I don't mind waiting for something if it's worth it. In fact, I'm a big fan of delayed gratification.'

He wasn't talking about the wreck. She knew that and he knew that, and for a second they stared at one another in silence and then she cleared her throat. 'Well, thank you for that. It was really kind of you.'

'It was my pleasure.' He held her gaze. 'So are you interested in going back down?'

It was a bad idea. Clearly it would be better, safer, to refuse, which meant there was only one possible response to that question. She took a deep breath. 'Yes,' she said.

After lunch on the yacht, it was time to dive again. This time, she remembered to take some photographs. Thank goodness for digital cameras, she thought as she zoomed in on the coral stretching over the wreck's hull. Swapping to the video camera, she felt her heartbeat slow. It was so calm down here away from dry land. So easy to forget that the real world even existed.

Chase tapped her on the arm, and, putting down the camera, she glanced round and saw that he was pointing to a striped sergeant major snuffling along the seabed. She started to follow him and then out of the corner of her mask, she saw it. A turtle propelling itself forward into the wreck using its paddle like flippers. She twisted in the water to watch it and then kicked forward. She had to get a picture.

A hand clamped around her arm. Chase was beside her, his eyes narrow beneath the mask. She pointed at the turtle but, shaking his head, he jerked his thumb towards the surface. She frowned, then reluctantly returned the signal and, still holding her arm, he guided her back up to the boat. As she climbed back on deck, he ripped off his mask and turned to face her.

'What the hell do you think you're playing at?' His deep voice was soft but there was a dangerous undertone that made the two remaining crew members scuttle to the other end of the boat. Gone was the easy intimacy and teasing smile of earlier, now his expression was as hard and inaccessible as the rock on his company's logo.

'You should have let me know if you wanted to go look at something, or do you not understand the meaning of dive buddy?'

He was talking about the turtle. 'Yes, of course I do,' she protested.

'Really?' The ice in his voice made her flinch inwardly. 'Because, for me, every dive is a contract, a duty of care for your buddy's safety.'

'I agree.'

'So, what, you just forgot?' His lip curled. 'Or were all the pretty fish too distracting for you?'

'No.' She was shaking her head. 'That's not how it was.' Fighting to keep her voice steady, she started to explain what had happened but he cut across her.

'It's exactly how it was.' And nothing was going to persuade him otherwise. She could see that in his eyes, in the hard, uncompromising set of his jaw. 'You're my buddy. You say you know what that means but it was just words because you didn't follow through.' She felt a prickling heat spread over her face as his eyes narrowed on her.

'You know, this isn't some dive pool, Jemima. This is the ocean and I don't dip my toe in it with anyone who isn't on the same page as me when it comes to understanding what they are responsible for. You can't just opt

out when you feel like it. You made a commitment—'
He broke off, his hand tightening around his mask.

Pain, a pain that had nothing to do with him, an old pain that was never far from the surface, fuelled her anger.

'You didn't give me a chance to—'

'To what? Prove me wrong? And what if you hadn't? What if I was right?' His voice was still fierce, but beneath the anger there was a rawness and a depth of passion that shocked her. 'Then it would all be too little too late.' He stopped, his beautiful mouth taut against his teeth. 'Do you know exactly how very little it takes to lose everything? No, of course, you don't. You're just a child, a stupid, thoughtless child.'

She stared at him, her heart sliding free of its moorings, stunned by the intensity of his fury. Even though the sun was hot on her back she felt cold inside her wetsuit. 'I'm not a child, and I do understand, and next time—'

'There's not going to be a next time.' A muscle jumped in his jaw. 'I don't do second chances because I spend every working day calculating risk, Jemima, and what you call second chances I call preventable accidents. And the consequences of those accidents are far reaching and devastating in ways I hope you never have to experience.'

His words hit her straight in the solar plexus like the kick of a horse, and there were tears in her eyes quite suddenly. It was a decade ago now but she could still remember sitting in that small, stifling room in the courthouse when the coroner had read out the verdict of accidental death. This, though, was a more accurate verdict because her father's death had been preventable.

By her.

Only she hadn't followed through then either. She had given up, walked away—no, make that crept away. And afterwards, she had only seen him that one last time.

She was suddenly afraid she would be sick.

'This was a mistake.' His face was shuttered, voice expressionless. 'My mistake. I thought you understood what was at stake but you don't, and I don't have people around me who don't understand the consequences of their actions. Particularly in the ocean.'

There was a long silence.

'I'm going to finish up here.' Chase glanced over his shoulder to where the crew were staring pointedly out to sea. 'I'll get someone to drop you back at the house.'

She stared after him, her chest splitting with a pain that had everything to do with him and nothing to do with him, a pain she would always have to shoulder because once again she had failed to follow through.

Back on the *Miranda*, Chase stalked into his cabin and slammed the door shut. He tossed his phone onto the bed and sat down, and then almost immediately got to his feet and began pacing round the room, his heart pounding out a drum roll of frustration and disbelief.

He kept a dry boat. Alcohol and diving were not just incompatible, they were a dangerous combination and he made no apologies about mandatory drug testing for the crew. Right now, though, he could have done with a glass of whisky. Or maybe a bottle, just something that would take the edge off his tension.

His jaw tightened.

It was her fault that he was feeling like this. Jemima had broken the rules. Worse, he had broken his own rules, inviting her out for a day of diving for no other reason than because he wanted to. Just as he had wanted to stay sitting there with her at breakfast. Talking. Eating. Catching her eye. Because it reminded him of all the things he had forced himself to forget. The kind of intimacies that went further than sex.

Catching sight of his reflection in the mirror, he stopped pacing. For a moment, he stood there, breathing unsteadily, replaying the moment when he had checked her buoyancy vest. It had taken every ounce of willpower he had not to lean in and press his lips against the soft hairs at the nape of her neck.

He jerked his head back, his gaze darting to the mirror. But it wasn't his reflection looking back at him now. It was Jemima, her grey eyes wide, not with hunger, but shock and misery.

Swearing softly, he turned away.

She was soft and sweetly serious, he thought, remembering her slightly incoherent outburst the night before. It wasn't so much what she'd said that had surprised and unsettled him. It was because he sensed that she wasn't just talking about the wider world but something deeper, something intrinsically personal to her. He had seen it in that quiver to her mouth. Something, most likely someone, had hurt her. Was that why she was here, thousands of miles from home? Was she running away from the hurt?

There was no point in running, he wanted to tell her. Pain was like your shadow. You could never escape it. You could lose yourself in drink or drugs temporarily, but to have any kind of life the only solution was to shut the door on your feelings. All of them.

That was the price you had to pay.

But that wasn't right for someone like Jemima, he thought, picturing her small, tense face, hearing the emotion in her voice as she talked about saving the world. He didn't know how old she was but in that moment she had seemed young, too young to be around someone as jaded as him.

She was also not his problem.

Not his problem, he repeated. What he needed was some fresh air to clear his head. Maybe stretch his legs. Which was how, an hour later, he found himself standing outside her cabin.

Of course, he'd told himself he was just going to say goodbye and no hard feelings, act like a grown-up, right up until he stopped in front of her door, but now that he was here he felt as if every second since he'd walked into Joan Santos's house had been leading up to this moment.

He took a slow breath, then tightened his hand into a fist and rapped his knuckles against the wood.

"One Minute" Survey

You get up to **FOUR** books <u>and</u> a Mystery Gift...

See inside for details.

YOU pick your books –
WE pay for everything.
You get up to FOUR new books and a Mystery Gift...
absolutely FREE!
Total retail value: Over $20!

Dear Reader,

Your opinions are important to us. So if you'll participate in our fast and free "One Minute" Survey, YOU can pick up to four wonderful books that WE pay for when you try the Harlequin Reader Service!

As a leading publisher of women's fiction, we'd love to hear from you. That's why we promise to reward you for completing our survey.

IMPORTANT: Please complete the survey and return it. We'll send your Free Books and a Free Mystery Gift right away. And we pay for shipping and handling too! *We pay for EVERYTHING!*

Try **Harlequin® Desire** and get 2 books featuring the worlds of the American elite with juicy plot twists, delicious sensuality and intriguing scandal.

Try **Harlequin Presents® Larger-Print** and get 2 books featuring the glamourous lives of royals and billionaires in a world of exotic locations, where passion knows no bounds.

Or TRY BOTH!

Thank you again for participating in our "One Minute" Survey. It really takes just a minute (or less) to complete the survey… and your free books and gift will be well worth it!

If you continue with your subscription, you can look forward to curated monthly shipments of brand-new books from your selected series, always at a discount off the cover price! Plus you can cancel any time. So don't miss out, return your One Minute Survey today to get your Free books.

Pam Powers

CHAPTER SIX

'JUST A MINUTE.'

He heard movement inside the room and then the door opened and Jemima was there. She had changed out of the wetsuit and her body looked stiff beneath the blouse and shorts. Behind her glasses, her eyes looked suspiciously bright. His stomach twisted. As if she'd been crying. Over her shoulder, he could see her bag at the end of the bed.

'I'm nearly ready,' she said quickly. Her voice was strained. It betrayed too much, and he felt something claw at him inside. 'I just need to grab a few last things.'

Chase stared at her, his pulse beating a drum roll through his limbs. If he had any sense he would say goodbye right about now and walk away, but...

A memory of Jemima, standing naked in front of him, quivering like a wildflower in the moonlight, slid into his head overlaid with that flush of rose pink that stained her cheeks wherever she met his gaze. Instantly, any sense he had was forgotten.

'That's not why I'm here.' He hesitated. It had been a long time since he'd had to explain his behaviour to anyone. Who would he explain himself to? Robyn. His COO. But also there was nothing to explain because he had made sure that he always did the right thing.

Only he hadn't done the right thing with Jemima. In fact he had done the very opposite, letting his imagination override what was actually happening.

'About earlier, on the dive boat. I might have over-reacted.' He frowned, remembering how, in the moment, panic had put an aggressive edge on his voice. 'Actually, I know I did. It's what I do. My business is all about worst-case scenarios and any dive is chock-full of those.'

And not just dives. Life was dangerous and unpredictable and unfair and devastatingly cruel. Heart contracting, he thought back to the face of the police officer who had told him about the crash. She had been so young; around Jemima's age probably. He could remember the tremor in her voice and how she couldn't meet his gaze. Her eyes kept flickering away from his face as if it hurt to look at him.

He could feel Jemima's gaze on his face now.

'It happens all the time. Just last month I came across this boat, anchored up, guys on deck leaning over the sides. We got closer and it turned out they'd lost a couple of divers.'

His pulse slipped sideways, pulled on an unseen current. Of all the possible explanations, why had he picked that one to share? But it was too late to backtrack.

'Apparently it was supposed to be a short, deep dive and the guys who went down were very experienced. Only they hadn't resurfaced. The skipper went to take a look but there was no sign of them. It was only when he got back up they noticed that neither of the divers had taken their digital compasses.'

He could tell from the look on her face that Jemima understood the significance of that fact. How without a compass it would be near impossible to reorient yourself to the position of the dive boat.

'All of us were just staring at the water and then one of my crew spotted this tiny glint of silver way, way off in the distance. It was a good kilometre from the dive boat but we went to investigate and there they were. One of them was wearing a watch. He was aiming it at the sun. That's what we saw.'

'Were they okay?'

'They were a bit shaken. But they were fine.'

She bit into her lip, her face suddenly taut. 'How did you know they were in trouble? The people on the boat.'

Because he was looking for it. His ribs squeezed around his lungs so that it was suddenly hard to catch his breath. It was the least he could do after having failed so devastatingly to see what was going on right in front of him.

He shrugged. 'Something felt off, you know?'

'And you were right,' she said quietly. 'You were right about earlier too. I did get distracted. I didn't follow through.' Her mouth quivered. 'I should finish packing.' He felt a spasm of panic and pain as she started to close the door.

'No, that's not why I told you that story.' He took a step forward. 'I was trying to explain why I overreacted.' Although that barely scratched the surface. 'But the fact is that anyone can get distracted.'

'Not you.'

'Yes, of course me. I went down to the harbour to collect medical supplies and instead I ended up trying to rent you a bike.' He thought that might make her smile but instead she wrapped her arms around her torso as if she was cold. It made him want to reach out and hold her. But what right did he have to touch her now? And she would be leaving soon. Dive or no dive, that was the plan. Only did it have to stay the plan?

'Jemima, please.' He took a deep breath. 'Look, I shouldn't have spoken to you like that. I guess I was worried because you're my guest and I feel responsible for you.'

'Well, you're not.' Her mouth quivered. 'We barely know each other.'

His fingers flexed. But he wanted to know her. And he didn't want her to leave. 'I came down to say goodbye when what I should be saying is sorry. And I am. Sorry. For what I said. For how I said it.' He took another step towards her. 'Please, I'd like you to stay.'

He watched her bite down on the inside of her lip. 'I thought you didn't do second chances.'

His chest tightened. Earlier, with panic and anger blazing through him, that had been true. Now though, staring down into her wide grey gaze, he was willing to make an exception.

'I don't do one-night stands either. But I couldn't walk away from you that night.'

There was a moment of heavy silence, the kind that smothered all sound.

He could see her pulse beating in her throat. 'I didn't want you to walk away.' Her voice brushed against his cheek like the wing of a gull and he stared at her, rooted to the spot by the storm in her eyes.

'And now,' he said hoarsely. 'Do you want me to walk away now?'

He held his breath as she reached up and rested her hand against his chest. 'No.'

Chase stared down into Jemima's face, his pulse leaping through his ribs to where her hand rested against his shirt, shivery pleasure dancing across his skin. He held his breath as she touched his cheek, her fingers grazing the stubble along his jaw, conscious only of the hammering of his heart and of his need, a need he saw reflected in her glazed grey eyes.

This was madness, he thought, distant alarms sounding in the margins of his brain. This could only make everything more complicated than he wanted it to be. But he couldn't move; couldn't look away.

And then she clasped his face in her hands in a jerky movement, and as her mouth found his he knew that only she could quiet this humming in his veins and he reached for her, locking his hand in her hair, pressing the other against the indent on her back, urging her closer.

He felt her breath shudder against his mouth and she moved against him, pressing her pelvis against his groin.

From somewhere on the boat, there was the sound of

voices, a shout of confirmation. Her startled eyes met his and he saw her confidence falter and he stood there, not moving, not breathing, awash with panic and fear lest she call a halt.

His body was shaking inside, clamouring for her from head to toe but he waited, and he would walk away if he had to, but a second passed and then another, and then she stood on tiptoe to reach closer, hands fluttering to his shoulders, fingers biting into the muscles, kissing him blindly, greedily.

The walls swam around him as she started to pull him into the bedroom.

'Wait,' he muttered against her mouth, turning to kick the door shut, and then she was pulling him close again.

His need for her swelled up inside him. He wanted her, wanted her so badly, had been wanting her again from the moment he woke to find her gone. And now she was here, in his arms, her soft mouth working on his already overheated senses.

'I've been thinking about this for days,' he murmured against her mouth, 'thinking about you.'

'I've been thinking about you too,' she said hoarsely. His teeth clenched as she slid her hands down over his body, down to where his erection was pushing against his shorts. As she cupped the weight of him, he sucked in a sharp breath.

It would all be over far too soon if he let her keep touching him like that.

Batting away her hand, and driven by the hunger uncoiling in the pit of his stomach, he scooped her up into his arms and carried her over to the bed.

He reached down and touched the swell of her breasts, feeling the taut nipples, his hands trembling and clumsy with a hunger he had never experienced. He felt feverish, drunk almost with lust and relief that it was happening. Leaning forward, he kissed her again, slowly, deeply, tasting her excitement, her nerves, her need.

'I want you,' he whispered.

Her eyes met his and he could see the glitter in them, see the flush of heat in her cheeks. She touched his face, his mouth, her trembling fingers hot against his skin.

'Then take me,' she said, and the need in her voice was like a flint to the steel in his shorts.

Blood pounding like a wrecking ball inside his head, he stripped off his top and threw it onto the floor and then pushed his shorts down past his straining erection. Her eyes widened, the pupils dilating; he could see her pulse leaping at him through the delicate skin of her throat, and, holding his gaze, she reached down and began to unbutton her blouse.

Still holding his gaze, she let it slide from her shoulders. He stared down at her breasts, his body hardening, hypnotised by the taut, quivering nipples, and then he leaned forward and licked first one swollen tip, and then the other.

Her fingers bit into his haunches. 'Chase…' She made his name last three syllables as he licked a path up the curve of her neck to her pink, parted lips.

'Jemima…'

Desire drowning him, he lowered his mouth and kissed her again, pushing her back onto the bed. He tugged off her shorts, taking her panties with them, then took a step backwards, the cool air between them just enough to keep things from ending much too quickly.

She was naked now except for her glasses and, staring down at her, he gritted his teeth. She was beautiful. And she was his. To touch. To stroke. To taste.

Sliding his hands beneath her bottom, he pulled her closer, parting her thighs so that he could settle between them. For a moment, he breathed in her scent, his thumbs caressing her silken skin, and then he tilted her so that she was more open to him and traced a line with his tongue between her legs.

She jerked forward, lifting her hips, and he felt her fingers tangle in his hair as she moaned softly, shivers of pleasure or excitement or passion scudding across her skin in time to the sweep of his tongue.

A grating sound rose in the back of his throat. He loved the taste of her. Loved the noises she was making as she started to move against him, arching upwards, her body spasming and twisting frantically like a puppet on a string, hands flexing against his shoulders.

She cried out, and he felt her shudder, and shudder and shudder.

He shifted up the bed, his mouth finding hers, and she gripped his arm weakly, her fingers closing around the hard length of him, guiding him inside her.

Heat roared through him. He was so close now; his body tensed, the fog of unfocused thoughts that might loosely be described as his brain suddenly clearing, and he pulled back and out.

'I don't have any protection on me.'

She stared at him, her grey eyes wide and unfocused. 'I don't have any either.' Her breathing was still ragged.

'They're in my cabin, I'll go and—'

But she was shaking her head, pulling him closer, and now it was too late to stop, he didn't want to stop, he couldn't stop. He was so desperate for release, but he didn't ever take risks when it came to sex, and, reaching up, he pulled Jemima underneath him so that the hard length of his erection was pressing into the softness of her belly.

'Yes,' he muttered as she wrapped her legs tightly around his waist and then he was moving against her in an ever quickening, mindless rhythm and the friction kept building, growing stronger and sharper.

He lunged forward and, groaning, he juddered against her with convulsive liquid force.

For a moment he couldn't move. He just lay there, listening to the slap of the waves against the side of the boat, his heart pounding, his breath tearing his throat, her breath hot against his chest. Beneath him, he could feel the aftershocks of her orgasm still pulsing through her in waves and, shifting his weight off her body, he rolled onto his side, drawing her into his arms, aware of the slick wetness on her skin and his.

'I'm sorry,' she said after a moment.

Her face was pressed into his chest but he heard the catch in her voice and he turned so that he was on his side facing her. He could see the pulse at the base of her neck beating wildly. 'For what?'

But he knew what. He knew that she was remembering the moment when she had guided him into her body without protection. There was a stretch of silence and then she looked up at him. 'I don't know what I was thinking.'

'Thinking?' He ran his hands over her body, leaning back slightly so he could admire her small breasts. 'I don't think either of us were thinking.' That was certainly true for him. His body, his brain, his whole being had been consumed with one *un*thinking purpose.

He placed his open palm against her face. 'We weren't prepared. Either of us.' That was an understatement, he thought, gazing down at her flushed face.

She bit her lip. 'It shouldn't have happened. I shouldn't have let it happen. But I don't regret it.' She seemed genuinely confused by that statement and he laughed softly.

'I don't regret it either.' He pulled her closer and felt her body shudder as her nipples brushed against his chest.

'Are you sure? I mean, you didn't…it wasn't—'

'It was.' Although it had happened faster than anticipated, a sudden, unstoppable quickening of his, like a seam tearing. He couldn't have held back another second. He hadn't lost it like that in years, possibly ever. No matter how good the sex had been in his previous relationships, he'd always managed to pace himself so that there was time to put on a condom. But he had lost control with Jemima.

And yet he hadn't been lying when he said he didn't have any regrets.

Then again...

His gaze slid hungrily along the curve of her bottom. He'd had sex with her, twice now, so why did he still feel hungry? It made no sense.

Or perhaps it made a kind of limited sense. *Yes*, thanks to this encounter, one night had turned into one night plus, but it all felt a little rushed; tantalising rather than satisfying. Like being invited back to a banquet only to have all the delectable dishes whisked away after just a few mouthfuls.

And before he got a chance to sample the dessert menu. His gaze travelled over her body to where her nipple was playing peekaboo beneath the hair that had fallen forward across her breast. Next time, he'd make sure they made it to desserts.

Next time?

Confused by the tangle of emotion that thought produced, he leaned forward and kissed her lightly on the shoulder, and then, loosening his arms, he shifted to the edge of the bed.

'Are you hungry? Because I'm starving.'

Hungry.

Jemima stared at Chase dazedly as he stood up. Her whole body was still quivering inside, tingling from the aftershocks of her orgasm and the stunned realisation that she and Chase had gone from a one-night stand to whatever it was called when you hooked up for the second time, only now he was talking about food.

As he turned towards her she had to force herself not to stare at his beautiful, naked body.

'I don't know.' Frankly, she didn't care, but Chase was already reaching down to pick up his clothes.

'Pick something.' The coolness in his voice scraped against her skin. 'Gianluca and his staff are all cordon-bleu-trained so they can pretty much knock up anything you want. I'm thinking steak and chips.'

Her head was spinning. She had no idea what was happening. In the past, with her boyfriends, sex had always happened after a couple of dates, more than a couple in some cases. With Chase sex had been the end-game, the finishing line. Only now they'd had sex again.

But what did that mean? Did it mean anything?

She didn't know the answer to either of those questions. She just knew that the whole point of a one-night stand was that it only happened once and she had messed that up. Just as she always seemed to mess up everything to do with men and relationships. And now she was in a no-man's-land. Except there was a man and he was half naked.

'I'll go tell the galley.'

'No, I don't think that's a good idea.' She sat up and his gaze flattened into a slant of green. For a split second she stared at him in silence, trying to clear her head, trying to understand the look in his eye. A look that didn't seem to match the coolness in his voice. It was as if he wanted her but didn't want her.

He raised an eyebrow. 'So not steak and chips?'

She felt a tremor of panic. The cabin felt suddenly

tiny and claustrophobic and her throat felt suddenly too tight so that it was hard to catch her breath.

This was exactly why she had left last time. The confusion and awkwardness of post-coital interaction. This not being sure what he was thinking. Not being sure what she was even thinking.

'I don't care about the steak and chips. I'm talking about this.' Conscious of her naked body in comparison to his semi-clothed one, she bent down and began picking up her clothes from the floor. 'You and me. Look, just because we slept together—'

'Twice,' he interrupted her quietly.

Her fingers curled into fists. 'Just because we slept together again doesn't mean I want to have dinner with you.'

'You did last night.'

'That was different. It wasn't planned,' she protested.

'And this was?' He glanced back at the bed.

'No.' She blinked. It wasn't planned, and yet it had felt inevitable, inescapable, necessary. She felt exhaustion pressing down on her, heavy and stifling like a storm about to break. 'I don't want to talk about it.'

'Oh, that's right. I'd forgotten. No questions. No conversation.' His face was expressionless, but there was an edge to his voice. 'That's why you did a runner last time. But we're on a boat in the middle of the ocean so that's going to be a little harder to pull off, don't you think, Jemima?'

'Not as hard as you think,' she snapped. Hating that she couldn't keep the shake out of her voice, she snatched up the remainder of her clothes and walked stiffly towards the bathroom and shut, then locked the door.

As solutions went it wasn't particularly effective, she realised a moment later. She couldn't stay in the bathroom for ever, but neither did she want to keep having that horrible conversation with Chase.

It was all such a mess, she thought as she buttoned up her blouse.

And it was her fault. She had drawn a clear line in the pink sand the morning after the night before but then she had to go and blur the boundaries between them by staying in his house and going diving with him. It had been a stupid thing to do but then, when it came to men, she was stupid, and weak.

Look at how she'd let Nick treat her. And he wasn't the first.

Her throat tightened and she felt suddenly close to tears. The whole point of coming to Bermuda was to do things differently. To be different. And with Chase, that had happened. She had felt an intense physical attraction to him and acted on it without thought of even the immediate future.

Without any kind of thinking at all.

And it had been scary, but also empowering, only now she was back where she started. Letting herself be buffeted along by stronger currents like those two divers. Repeating the mistakes of the past when what she should be doing was breaking free of them. She pictured her father's face, the skin red and flaky, his bony cheeks covered in patchy grey stubble. Only that would mean facing up to who she was, and what she'd done.

There was no sound on the other side of the door and she unlocked it cautiously, but the bedroom was empty. She felt both relief and a disappointment that made her heart feel as if it were being squeezed hard by a huge fist. And the irrationality and hypocrisy of that made her want to scream.

She was losing her mind. She needed to get off this boat and as far away from Chase Farrar as possible. Grabbing her bag, she yanked open the door—and stopped.

Chase was sitting on the floor opposite the cabin.

Her stomach twisted with shock and another kind of relief entirely. The stupid kind that made her whole body fill with light, and made her thoughts spiral towards the impossible.

'What are you doing?'

'Waiting for you.' The huskiness in his voice brought a rush of heat to her cheeks. 'I was worried but—' glancing at her bag, he got to his feet '—I see I didn't need to be.' Eyes narrowing, he stalked past her into the bedroom. 'What? No note? How disappointing.'

As she watched him turn, her heart began to pound fiercely. 'Why are you bringing that up?'

'Because that's what you do, isn't it?'

'And now you can see why,' she countered. 'It's a whole lot easier than trying to talk to you.'

'Oh, now you want to talk. Because earlier you preferred to sulk in the bathroom.'

As he stalked towards her, she felt her whole body tighten. Twenty minutes ago their bodies had collided on that bed, driven by a mutual hunger that was as intense as the storm that hit the island last night. Now that storm was blowing in a completely different direction. 'I wasn't sulking. I was upset.'

Jaw tightening, his gaze held hers. 'Yeah, because we had sex again.' His voice was so cold that for a moment it seemed to freeze her brain and she couldn't take in what he was saying. And then she did.

'No, that's not why I was upset.' Except it was, in part, and, looking into his eyes, seeing the emotion smouldering there, she knew that he had heard it in her voice.

His gaze burned into her face. 'I'm sorry to disappoint you, Ms Friday.'

'And, of course, this is only about you.' Now she felt a flicker of anger. Not just with Chase but with herself for thinking that a one-night stand might change the essential dynamic between her and every man she had ever met, except her brother. 'You know, I don't know why I thought this would be any different. Why you'd be different.' Her voice came out scratchy.

Why I'd be any different, she might have said.

Chase frowned, his gaze suddenly intent on her face. 'Different from what?'

Feeling trapped, she looked away, a lump forming in her throat.

'Different from what?' he said again.

He was standing too close, his hard, muscular body radiating power and authority, and something that felt oddly like concern. 'It's complicated.' She wished he would leave but he just stood there, waiting, his body blocking her in, and she knew that he wasn't about to let her go this time. Not without her answering his question first.

'This is why I wrote that note,' she said finally, avoiding his eyes. 'Because I don't know how to do this. I thought I did but I don't. You see, I lied to you. Before. I told you I didn't do relationships. That wasn't true.'

She felt his green gaze narrow on her face. 'You have a boyfriend.'

'No.' Finally she looked up at him. 'Not any more. But I did. His name is Nick. He cheated on me. That's why I came to Bermuda. Why I'm having this holiday. My brother and sister thought I should get away. Go somewhere new. Be someone different. Let my hair down. They sorted it all out, and I went along with it because—'

'They're a force of nature.' He finished the sentence for her.

'Yes, but then I met you.' Her pulse skipped forward as she remembered that moment at the harbour when he had swaggered out from behind the counter. 'And I wanted you, and you made me want to be this cool, impulsive, wild woman so I let you think that was who I was.'

He said nothing, just stared at her, waiting.

'It all seemed so easy in the moonlight but then when I woke up I panicked.' Had she been the expert she claimed to be, she would have casually informed him the night before that she had an early start. Instead she had ended up creeping around in the dawn-lit cabin, terrified that he would wake at any moment and the spell would be broken, and that night of fantasy would be lost and forgotten among the awkward goodbyes.

'I know I acted like it was something I do all the time, but I've never had a one-night stand and I didn't know how it worked.' She swallowed. 'It was so perfect, I didn't want to ruin it, so I got up and left. And it would have been fine if we never met again.'

She saw him swallow, saw a muscle tighten in his jaw.

'Only we did. And it was too late to tell you that I'd never done anything like that before. But then you knocked on my door and I realised that it didn't matter what I told you because I knew the truth. I knew that it wasn't fine. That I still wanted you, and I don't want to feel like this, but I can't seem to stop myself.'

But she did stop now. Lowering her face, she breathed out unsteadily. She had never admitted half as much to anyone but then she had never felt so physically connected to any man.

'And I feel the same.' Pulse trembling, she looked up to see his pupils flare. 'So why run from it?' he said hoarsely.

Her belly clenched, his question stabbing at her, slicing through her defences.

'I don't.'

'Yes, you do. It's like you said. You know the truth. We both do.' His green gaze burned into hers. 'So what's the point of running? Or hiding? Or pretending that you don't want this?'

Heart thudding, she gazed up into his beautiful, sculpted face, her insides tightening, her body betraying her, the raw, sexual challenge of his words pounding through her like a drum roll. For a moment neither of them spoke or moved, and then he reached out, tugged gently at the band in her hair, and she stared at him transfixed, unable to move, helpless, fascinated by his touch.

'You came to let this down.'

As her hair tumbled loose, he twisted the blonde strands, winding them into a rope as Rapunzel had done so that the prince could climb up the tower to rescue her. But instead he used it as a pulley to draw her closer to him. 'To have fun, and go diving. And I get that this is all new to you. But that's not a reason to leave. So why not stay here with me on the *Miranda*? Just until the beach house is fixed? I have an event in New York coming up but other than that I'm all yours.'

It was just a phrase, she told herself, but his words made her body ache.

He untwisted her hair and let it hang loose. 'I can make all those things you want happen.'

A moment earlier she had wanted him to leave. Now her heart was beating against her ribs, his suggestion catching the sunlight like the divers' watches, pulling her in. This was only supposed to be a day trip. But then this was only supposed to be a one-night stand and what he was suggesting would mean being here on the *Miranda* for several days. The thought sent a fast twitch down her spine. Was that wise? She had already let it go further than she'd planned.

Then again there was still an end date, and it wasn't as if Chase were proposing marriage. Like her, he wanted to have fun. A pulse of heat pirouetted across her skin. So why walk away now? Why not have fun with him? And if she spent a little longer having fun out here with Chase, then maybe back in England she would be less likely to return to her old, bad habits.

'Is that what you want?'

She could see the dark flush in his cheekbones and his eyes were full of heat, but she needed to hear him say it.

'Yes,' he said simply, and he took the bag from her hand, tossed it onto the floor. She didn't say anything. She just stared at him, her heart pounding, and then she sidestepped past him and shut the door. As she turned to face him, he crossed the room in two strides and kissed her hungrily, his mouth drawing the heat from hers, his hands gripping her waist and pulling her back towards the bed.

CHAPTER SEVEN

PRESSING HER FACE against the submersible window, Jemima was lost for words, her mind empty, the questions and uncertainties of the last few days soothed away by the view through the glass. Only this time it wasn't just the sea life that was mesmerising but the water itself, she thought as the sunlight slipped away and the colour palette moved through a light curaçao to a bruised blue.

'What do you think?' Chase's voice made her jump and she turned to find him watching her, his green gaze shimmering as it met hers.

'I think it's very cool,' she said carefully.

He tipped his beautiful head back and laughed. 'I know, it's a bit of a toy, but it does serve a purpose. It means we can check out deeper sites without having to send divers down. Although, to be honest, we probably wouldn't even use the submersible until we locate a suitable wreck.'

'But how do you know it's suitable if you haven't taken a look?'

He turned towards her and she found herself trying

to take in his expression, his features, just as she had been doing ever since she had agreed to this fling. Because it didn't matter that some things had the feel of a relationship—the shared breakfasts, the long afternoons spent in bed, that intense pull of attraction that shimmered around them like a heat haze. None of it was heading anywhere. None of it was permanent.

The snatch of a song about summer flings echoed inside her head, and she glanced up through the glass bubble, her gaze following a school of silvery Bermuda chub.

It wasn't summer but fling was the best word to describe her 'relationship status' with Chase. She liked the idea that she was jumping into something new, or diving, even. And as with diving there was that shock of entering another state of being. But it was a good shock. Better than good, it was perfect for her life right now. She had promised Holly and Ed that she would have fun and she was having fun.

Although being the nerd she was, she had done a little covert research on the Internet just to reassure herself and it turned out that there were rules about holiday flings; thankfully she was following most of them.

She knew why she wanted to have a fling. She and Chase were on the same page. Plus there was zero chance of them dating long-term under different circumstances so there were already natural boundaries in place. And, finally, they were practising safe sex. Her face grew warm as she remembered how close she had come to letting him stay inside her that first day on the *Miranda*.

Safe in some ways.

The obvious ways.

But there were other hazards and unforeseen consequences that no condom could protect against.

Like having to accept the unlikelihood of her ever finding a man who liked pleasing his partner sexually as much as Chase did. A man who was happy to take the lead, to be guided, to wait, to celebrate her hunger while satisfying his own.

A beat of heat danced over her skin. She'd had sex with her previous boyfriends but mostly she had been too worried about their pleasure to think about her own. She was too shy to say what she wanted, what she liked. Truthfully, she hadn't known what she liked.

Until now.

With Chase.

And now she knew the difference between having sex and having good sex. No, make that sublime sex. A lick of heat flickered up inside her at the memory of his hands moving urgently across her body and his hardness clamped between her thighs. No one had ever touched her like that or made her feel so helpless, so hungry.

Locking her knees, she was suddenly aware that Chase was saying something to her. Hoping that the shifting light would hide the colour in her cheeks, she said quickly, 'Sorry, I missed that.'

'I was just saying that we have other equipment we can use before we send down the sub.'

'What kind of equipment?'

'That depends on the depth of the water. The deeper you go, the more pressure there is and in those cases we use a remotely operated vehicle. They can be operated from the surface and you can add in manipulator arms, high-res cameras, viewing monitors. Then there's metal detectors, light systems. It just means that we can check out the sites with as little interference as possible,' he added. 'That way we can minimise the impact on the marine life.'

Their eyes met and she remembered that argument they'd had in the kitchen what felt like a lifetime ago—although it was just a matter of days, she realised with shock. But then time seemed to work differently here in Bermuda. Or maybe it was him, she thought as his gaze moved over her.

He had tipped her life upside down so why not time?

'How did you get into this? Looking for treasure, I mean.'

There was a beat of silence and then he shrugged. 'I grew up near a lake that's basically the size of a sea. We had a boat—not like the *Miranda*, more of a dinghy, really. But we spent a lot of time on the water and you end up diving wrecks and I guess it fired my imagination. I've always had a very vigorous imagination,' he added softly.

His eyes rested on her face and she felt her mouth dry. She knew all about his imagination.

She nodded. 'Down here is like another world. I can see why being able to think creatively would be helpful.'

He smiled. 'Nice divert,' he said softly. 'But you're right. We come up against challenges all the time that you just don't get on land. We've even had to design equipment for specific problems, and that's exciting in another way. Here, take a look at this,' he said, shifting the joystick minutely, then holding it steady. Glancing down, she saw that they were floating directly above a vivid orange coral colony.

Her pulse quivered with excitement. There had to be at least thirty, maybe forty different species of coral down there.

She leaned forward, her gaze travelling along the wreck where it crouched on the seafloor like a huge, sleeping animal. It was the *San Amunia*, a Spanish galleon that had been caught in a hurricane off the coast of Bermuda in 1654 and sank with no survivors. The ship had been picked over by salvage teams and amateur hunters, but it was now serving a second purpose as a home for hundreds of different species.

Reaching up, she touched the glass. Privately she had been a little dismissive about the sub. Surely nothing could beat the immediacy of diving. But now that she was here, she could see that, although it was less hands-on, the bubble allowed for a three-hundred-and-sixty-degree experience so that you could see how the marine life interacted with each other rather than having a viewpoint that was limited by the size of your mask.

'It's really incredible. Thank you for taking me out.'

'I'm glad you're enjoying it. I only got it about a month ago so I haven't had much of a chance to use it, you know, with the weather and—'

A shadow moved over the bubble of glass and they both glanced up to watch a spotted eagle ray swooping smoothly through the water, more like a bird than a fish, its great fins rising and falling like wings, the tail spine trailing after it like a kind of reverse antenna.

'They look like they're flying,' she said softly.

'They do fly. Most rays do, I think. They launch themselves about six feet into the air. If I hadn't seen it I would never have believed it…it was astonishing.' He checked himself, 'There's footage on the Internet, if you're interested.'

He glanced away towards where the rays were foraging around the bottom of the wreck and her eyes fixed on the fine, pale hairs at the nape of his neck, a pulse beating high in her throat. Why had he swerved the conversation away from the personal to the generic? It was so swift and subtle she doubted most people would have noticed, but she did a similar thing when she didn't want to give something of herself away. Only she talked about her siblings. But what could Chase possibly want to keep to himself about spotted eagle rays?

She cleared her throat. 'Why do they do it? Why do they jump?'

'For fun.' He grinned. 'Or because they're trying to shake off the parasites that live in their gills.'

'Like chickens having a mud bath.'

Glancing over, he laughed softly and she felt the sound move through her, tangling inside, unravelling her. 'I'm not that familiar with chickens but it sounds feasible. I've heard lots of different theories. Some people think that the males do it during mating season. To get noticed by the females.'

She heard the inflection in his voice and a flicker of sensation skated across her skin, hot and sharp like a flame. Chase didn't need to do anything to get noticed. Even today, in faded shorts and with his hair falling across his forehead, his was the kind of beauty that made people forget what they were saying when they saw him.

And it wasn't just women. Men responded to it too; or maybe they simply responded to the intangible but unmistakable leader-of-the-pack aura of authority that was as much a part of him as those glittering green eyes.

Outside the bubble, the rays had disappeared from view, and she leaned forward to see if she could see another.

'He'll be back. That wreck is like an all-you-can-eat buffet.' He hesitated, then tapped the joystick. 'Would you like to have a go?'

'Me?' She frowned.

His eyes gleamed. 'Yes, you—unless there's a very tiny stowaway in here that I don't know about.'

She laughed then. 'Okay, yes. I would like that.' Her eyes darted around the cabin with its state-of-the-art dashboard. He might think of it as a 'toy' but just thinking about how much it cost made her nervous. 'But do you trust me?'

'I could ask you the same question.' His gaze held hers, steady and direct. 'I mean, just getting into a submersible involves a substantial amount of trust.'

Did she trust him? She thought back to how he had gone through the safety measures in place in case of an emergency: the four days' worth of air, extra food and water, the rescue sub at the ready. She knew Chase would never put her in danger, but then she realised with a jolt that she trusted him in other ways too. Which was a first with anyone she'd been intimate with. Aways before she'd felt that betrayal and hurt were inevitable just as a spinning coin must eventually fall on its side. But probably because theirs was a physical relationship with a limited shelf life, she felt as if there was not the same risk of hurt or disappointment.

A gear shifted inside her head, reversing her back to when they'd argued after having sex again and he had waited outside the cabin to see that she was all right. It was a moment of care that went outside the boundaries of the physical.

'I do trust you,' she said quietly.

He didn't react but the sudden intensity of his gaze made her feel something a lot more complicated than nervous.

'Then it's very simple—there are four thrusters that allow the sub to move in any direction. This is up, this is down, left and right. Now you try.' He lifted his hand and she took hold of the joystick. The leather was still warm from his grip and for a moment she lost concentration, imagining that same hand warming her body. Very specific parts of her body.

The sub jerked forward, and now his hand covered hers. 'You're doing fine. Just ease into it. Like this. See? Good.'

'And how do you stop it?'

'That's a good question.' She felt his fingers splay over hers and the submersible stilled, hovering gently. 'Not one I would have thought of asking.'

'You wouldn't?' It seemed obvious to her.

He moved closer, his eyes resting on her face, the green layered with a dark heat she could feel inside her.

'Because when I'm with you, stopping is the last thing on my mind,' he said, his voice daring her in that dark, soft-edged way that made heat dance along her limbs and her skin prickle with a mix of panic and desire.

For a moment she couldn't breathe. Dizzily she stared up at him and then impulsively she leaned forward and kissed him, moaning softly as he kissed her back, his lips moving across hers, slowly, deliberately, tongue parting her lips in a sensual exploration that made her belly feel hot and tight with need.

She really was dizzy now. Her head was spinning. She blinked, bracing herself against the sea. No, actually, it was the submersible.

'Chase.'

He jerked backwards and Jemima's eyes met his, the pupils flaring with shock and a hunger that matched the need galloping through his body. Which would be fine except that they were five hundred feet under water in a bubble of air. Breathing out shakily, he moved the joystick fractionally and the sub slowed, then came to a quivering stop.

There was a flush of pink along her cheekbones. 'I don't remember anything about that in the safety protocol talk.'

He shook his head. 'No, I'm pretty sure kissing your co-pilot is not standard procedure.'

His heart thudded as she reached out and pressed

her hand flat against the front of his shorts, feeling the hard length of him. 'I think it might be time to go back up to the boat.'

'I think so too,' he said hoarsely.

They made it to the cabin. Just.

They didn't take off their clothes. As he opened the door to her cabin, she grabbed his hand and pulled him inside and he caught her by the waist, spinning her round and back against the door, bringing his mouth down on hers with a hunger that made her gasp. And then he was pushing her dress above her waist, sliding on a condom and thrusting into her, both of them still standing. It was fast and hard. Sex at its most basic and her climax was so intense that he had to hold her against him to keep her upright.

It was natural to feel this desperate, he told himself as he watched her sleep. There was a clock ticking. The credits were going to roll on this episode with Jemima as soon as the beach house was fixed. And she was feeling it too; that was why there was this tension between them and why he had snapped at her. So although it felt as if her talking about her ex had changed things between them, it was just that this wanting Jemima, wanting someone specific, hadn't happened in such a long time and it was knocking him off balance.

Why else would he have ended up telling her about those divers?

His spine tightened as he imagined their shock and terror as they broke through the surface. It made him remember Frida and his own shock and the agony of understanding that she was gone and that he was alone too. Only for him it was an aloneness that would last for ever.

And yet, being with Jemima in the sub all those metres below the surface he'd felt, not alone, but connected so that he had thought about telling her the truth. But then he had come to his senses.

She had got upset, and in the moment she had needed to share something about herself, and that was fine but there was no need to reciprocate.

Not outside bed anyway.

They spent the rest of the day relaxing. Or rather she relaxed on a sunlounger and Chase joined other members of the crew to hop the waves on his custom-built jet ski. Watching him perform a series of faultless back flips and barrel rolls, Jemima wondered drowsily if he ever ran out of energy. He seemed to have endless stamina.

Her eyes fixed on where he sat on the jet ski, his hair salt-tangled and bright in the sun's dazzle of clear gold, water trickling down his muscular torso. It didn't seem possible but she wanted him again, wanted him now.

Just as if he could hear her thoughts, Chase looked up at the yacht, his green gaze tearing into her, and she felt an excruciating, irresistible tug low in her pelvis. She could imagine his hands on her stomach, her hips, between her thighs.

Watching him turn the jet ski towards the *Miranda*, she felt her pulse leap in her veins. Soon she wouldn't have to use her imagination. That was the upside of this arrangement.

And the downside?

She bit into her lip. She wasn't allowing herself to think about that right now. She was living for the present. Enjoying every moment while she could. And there was a lot to enjoy, she thought, her stomach cartwheeling as Chase walked out onto the owner's deck.

'I thought we might head out to deeper water tomorrow.'

Looking up at him, Jemima frowned. 'I thought the sub only went down two hundred metres.'

They were lying in each other's arms, bodies twitching and spent.

When they'd returned to the cabin earlier, they had stripped and showered and she had taken him in her mouth with the water cascading down her back. Finally they'd made it to the bed. Capturing her wrists, he had lowered himself between her legs, taking his time, making her wait, waiting for her to beg.

And she had begged, crying out his name, rocking against his mouth, her body losing shape, weightless suddenly and adrift, thighs shaking as her orgasm hit.

'So you were listening to me earlier.' Lifting her chin, Chase kissed the corner of her mouth and worked his way to the other side. 'You're right, it does, but the *Eurybia* can go another three hundred metres.'

Five hundred metres. That was deep. Even just thinking about it made her feel breathless. Then again, she was still trying to catch her breath from before, she thought, nestling in closer to Chase. His name suited him. With his latent muscularity and smooth, tanned skin, there was something of a hunter about him.

Although she was as greedy for him as he was for her.

She had no words to describe what it was like to explore his beautiful body with such unthinking freedom, or how his touch made her feel, just that she felt happier than she could ever remember feeling, calmer too. And safe. Her heart slipped sideways a little. She had never felt safe before with any of the men she'd dated. She had always been on edge, waiting like Chicken Little for the sky to fall on her head. Except that made it sound as though her life was filled with drama.

And sometimes it was, but mostly it was less attention-grabbing, more quietly exhausting. A kind of slow-motion panicky treading of water to keep from going under, and a feeling of being incredibly alone.

Her throat tightened and she remembered Chase talking about the divers. Picturing the two men bobbing in a wide expanse of blue, that random glint of silver, she shivered.

'What's up?'

As Chase pulled her closer, she tilted her head back to meet his gaze. 'Nothing.'

He raised an eyebrow. 'I lost you there. Where'd you go?'

She reached up to touch his face, marvelling at the perfection of his bone structure and the smoothness of his skin.

'I was just thinking about those two divers you told me about. They were so lucky.'

Something flickered across his eyes like water moving beneath ice. 'What they were was arrogant and careless. They thought they were different. That those bad things they saw on the news only happened to other people. Bad things can happen to anyone given the right set of the wrong conditions.'

Like alcoholism crossed with pneumonia and a sudden, unseasonal but vicious drop in temperature, she thought, no longer on a superyacht but standing on a rainy London street near Piccadilly Circus where the lights were always on and you felt as if you were walking through a dream. But it was real. All of it was real.

Her chest tightened. Her father was a careless drunk. He forgot to eat. He had fallen and hurt himself multiple times. On one terrible occasion he had been beaten up and robbed on his way home.

And yet his death had been avoidable.

'You disagree?'

'No, you're right,' she said slowly. 'Bad things can happen to anyone, anywhere.' Especially when you did nothing to stop them from happening.

Glancing up, she found Chase watching her closely, his beautiful green eyes narrowed on her face as if he was trying to see inside her head. And she felt a sudden overwhelming urge to tell him the truth, to lay out her secrets before him, which wasn't just a bad idea, it basically was the very essence of a bad idea.

It was true that, since she had agreed to stay, they had talked about lots of things. But it was as if there were an electric fence humming between them. Aside from her telling him about her exes, any time anything got too deep or personal, they both backed away. And it didn't get any deeper or more personal than telling someone how you walked out on your alcoholic father. It was certainly too deep and personal for a holiday romance.

'Was it near here?' she said quietly. 'Where you found them?'

She felt the muscles in his arms tense and he stared down at her blankly, almost as if he were surprised to see her there, and then he shook his head. 'You don't need to worry. A lot of the crew are locals. They know where most of the strong currents are.' He said it casually, but there was an edge to his voice and she knew that as far as he was concerned the conversation was over even before he lowered his mouth to hers.

His hands were moving across her hips, now they were slipping between her thighs, his touch light, teasing, persuasive. In a moment, her skin would grow warm and she would start to melt, to dissolve into pure need.

Maybe she was reading too much into it. Maybe it was just that brush with almost-tragedy that had caught him off guard and reminded him of the power and unpredictability of the sea; the way a flat, calm surface could hide a riptide.

She caught his fingers, twisting them around her own. 'But shouldn't I know?'

There was a small, taut pause. His eyes narrowed a fraction. 'I thought you said you trusted me.'

'I do, but—'

'So trust me when I say that we won't be diving anywhere close to that site.'

He was right; she could trust him. *So row back,* she told herself. And yet—

Trust me.

She'd lost count of the number of times people had said that to her, and always they'd been lying. And with all those other people, it had mattered. The whole point of this fling with Chase was that it didn't need to matter. It was different. She was supposed to be different with him.

But this was her being different.

The old Jemima, the one she'd left back in England, would never be thinking like this. She would have looked the other way, and kept looking until she found her boyfriend having sex with a stranger in their bed.

Behind him, she could see the ocean rippling in the sunlight. It all looked so calm and welcoming, but sometimes the currents pulled you into dangerous waters anyway.

'It must have been horrible,' she said slowly. 'Stumbling across something like that.'

'Like what?' But he knew what. There was a wariness in his voice that hadn't been there before, the same rigidity in his body.

'Divers lost at sea. I can't stop thinking about it and I wasn't even there.'

He rolled over, taking her with him so quickly that she was on top of him before she had a chance to blink. 'I was just happy to help,' he said, and now he was moving his hands lightly down her back to the curve of her bottom, his touch making heat blossom deep inside her.

In another moment, she would lose the power to think, much less speak. It was something that had happened before, she realised, this reaching for one another. It was as if they had an unspoken agreement whenever there was a need to move away from tricky or unnecessarily personal topics of conversation. But why would he want to stop talking about those divers? Or the rays in the sub?

Gritting her teeth, she wriggled free and sat up. 'But it must have been upsetting,' she persisted.

'For them, sure.' His green eyes were dark with passion but as he reached up to cup her breasts with his hands, she could feel the tension in his body.

But why? She swallowed.

'So it wasn't your boat? Your divers?'

This time, he didn't move a muscle. She knew because she was watching him so closely she could see him breathing. But his expression hardened minutely.

'No, it wasn't my boat or my divers. Why would you ask me that?'

Staring up at him, she felt a tingly shiver dart down her spine. He was telling the truth. But he was also holding something back. That was the thing about dating so-called 'recovering' addicts: you got pretty good at being able to separate out all the strands; you could pick out the lies of omission from the distortions of the truth; the half-truths from the lies they had told themselves so often it felt as though they were real.

And all of it was tangled up with their shame and your guilt for having failed them. She felt suddenly exhausted, just as she used to feel when her dad was trying desperately to hide the truth from her, from himself.

'Because you seem so tense about it. I thought maybe—'

'If I'm tense, Jemima, it's because you're putting two and two together and making five.'

He tipped her off his lap and shifted to the edge of the bed and she stared at his back, her heart beating shakily. Blaming the other person was something else addicts did when they were trying to cover their tracks.

'That's not what I'm doing—' she protested.

But he cut her off. 'Then maybe you should rewind what you just said, because it sure sounded like that to me. I think I'm going to hit the gym. While I'm gone you might want to brush up on your pillow talk.'

'Pillow talk?' she echoed.

He was yanking on his clothes. 'Yeah, you know, the stuff people say to each other in bed in between having sex.'

People? Was that what she was to him? One of many. Faceless and interchangeable. The brusqueness of his words was like a slap to the face. 'I know what pillow talk is, Chase.'

'Apparently not. Or do you think all this is somehow going to make me horny?'

'What are you? Fifteen? I don't care if you're horny or not,' she said, grabbing at a T-shirt and yanking it over her head, her anger nudging past her shock at the sudden change in his mood. She felt as if she were driving a getaway car down a motorway. Her heart was ricocheting off her ribs, hands clenching so tightly that she thought the bones might shatter.

He stared down at her; the angles of his beautiful face looked as if they were cut from stone. There was a tiny, taut twist to one corner of his mouth. 'Lucky for you. Because you throwing accusations around—'

'I wasn't throwing accusations around. I was trying to understand you.'

'Then clearly you've missed the point of our arrangement, because I don't want to understand you and I sure as hell don't need you to understand me. Just to make things clear, this is about sex.'

The room went silent and still and for a second or two, Jemima just stared at him, her breath churning in her throat, his words echoing inside her head. She couldn't feel her hands, her body. It was the first time he had made her feel like that, like her other boyfriends had made her feel. Diminished and stupid. But unlike with them, she felt no sense of failure. Just a sudden, fierce anger that left her breathless.

'Yes, it is.' She rose from the bed like Venus rising from the waves. 'But you're the one who's missing the point if you don't also know that it's also about respect.'

There was a silence punctured only by the splintered sound of their breathing. She couldn't remember ever speaking to anyone like that. For a moment, she just sat there on her bed, listening to her heart banging in her chest.

'Mexico.'

His voice made her jump and she glanced over at where Chase stood facing her. There was no mistaking the tension in his body now. He looked as if he were bracing himself against the impact of some unseen, outsized wave.

'What about Mexico?'

Another silence, longer this time.

'You asked me where those divers got lost.' The

anger was gone. In fact, his voice was wiped of all emotion. 'It was off the coast of Mexico.'

Staring across the room at Jemima, Chase felt his chest tighten.

'Why didn't you just tell me that?' Her grey eyes found his, clear, puzzled, the anger that had lit them up moments earlier fading.

Because of this. Because in answering one question he had unleashed a wave of others. Only they were harder to answer. And each one would be more painful than the last.

'I didn't think you needed to know. I thought it would make things complicated. I knew you didn't want that. Neither of us did.'

He heard her breath quicken. 'Why would you being in Mexico complicate things?'

His head shuddered like a building in an earthquake. 'Because I was with my parents-in-law.'

Her face seemed to shrink. She sank back down on the bed and he could see that her legs were shaking. 'You're married?'

He shook his head. 'Not any more.' He could hear the finality in his words; she heard it too. He could tell from the way her body seemed to lose shape.

'What was her name?' she said quietly.

'Frida. I didn't tell you about her because—' His head was spinning, there were so many reasons, and yet weirdly he couldn't think of one.

'You don't have to explain. We don't have to talk. We can just sit here.' Jemima's voice cut across the panicky swirl of his thoughts and instantly he felt calmer. She was right. He didn't have to tell her anything, but for some reason he wanted to.

'She was their only child. They miss her especially around the anniversary of her—' The word stuck in his throat.

'When did it…? When did she…?'

'Eight years ago.' His chest tightened. He had never talked to anyone about the accident. Had never wanted to, but then this was the first time he had spoken Frida's name aloud to anyone outside his family and it seemed to loosen something inside him so that before he understood that he was doing it, he began talking about a past he had buried along with his wife.

'We met at college. When I dropped out, she still married me. For our honeymoon, we hired a yacht. Not like the *Miranda*. It was smaller but we both loved sailing. That's when we saw the rays.'

He hesitated, then cleared his throat.

'She got her law degree, joined a firm while I messed around on more boats. Then my dad got ill and I went to help out at his insurance firm, and I liked it. But I wanted to do things my way so I set up Monmouth Rock.'

Something strange was happening to his voice. It sounded different, almost as though it were being artificially generated.

'We started trying for a baby and she got pregnant really quickly. But then we lost the baby early before the first scan. And we were upset but we tried again, and she got pregnant again. And she miscarried. It kept happening. The doctors were doing all these tests and we talked about surrogacy but Frida wanted to keep trying.'

It had been the hardest thing that had never happened.

'By then the business was global and I was flying all over the world and it was hard for both of us. She was struggling. Not sleeping. She blamed herself even though it wasn't her fault. And then one day she told me she couldn't do it any more. She couldn't keep trying.'

It had been the worst moment of his life watching her despair. Or so he had thought then.

'So we stopped trying for about a year. She went on the pill. She changed her diet, started doing yoga and painting and we agreed that we would use a surrogate. We were looking into it when she got this bug and she was sick for days. It must have messed up the pill because about a month later she found out she was pregnant. And this time it stuck, and she was so happy. I was too.'

His chest tightened. There was no easy way to say what happened next. In fact, he'd always thought he didn't have the words, but glancing over to where Jemima sat clutching the sheet around her body, her gaze still, steady, unwavering, he said quietly, 'She was five months pregnant when she lost that baby.' There was a tiny silence. 'It was a girl.'

He felt as shocked now as he was then. Shocked too that he was telling Jemima.

'I'm so sorry, Chase.'

Her voice was so soft he wished he could just wrap

himself in it. But he didn't deserve to be comforted. He didn't deserve her sympathy.

'I had some time off but then I had to go back to work.' He frowned. 'I wanted to go back to work because I thought that if things got back to normal it would help. But it didn't. She was hardly eating. She'd stopped seeing her friends. I took her to the doctors and she was given anti-depressants but they made her drowsy. In the end I decided to take some more time off work. We had a house in upstate New York. I thought we could spend some time there, together. I was going to drive her, but I had to hand over things at work and it all took longer than I thought it would.'

He felt as if he were underwater. Every breath was being torn from his lungs. 'I was still at work when the police came to find me. Her car had spun off the road and hit a bunch of trees. She was killed instantly.'

For several seconds, every part of Jemima's mind was narrowed in on finding words that could take the pain out of Chase's voice and then she was unfolding her legs and moving towards him. She slid her arms around his body, feeling his grief, his loss bleed through her.

Seconds later, she felt his arms tighten around her.

'I'm so sorry,' she whispered against his chest. It wasn't enough, but it was what she was feeling and she wanted to give him her truth. That was her job as a 'witness' to that most private of emotions: grief.

'I'm so sorry that happened to you.'

She heard him swallow. 'It's not just me it happened to. Her parents are still so devastated.'

'And you're there for them.'

'And you think that makes me some kind of saint?' He loosened his grip; his beautiful face was taut. 'It's the least I could do after what I let happen to their daughter.'

'You didn't let anything happen,' she protested. 'It was an accident.'

'An accident is just what people say so that they don't have to feel responsible.'

Except he did feel responsible. Which was why he had reacted so strongly when she had swum after that turtle. The whole experience of losing his baby and wife in short succession had made him want to save people from themselves as fervently as she wanted to save the planet. She caught his hands. 'You weren't responsible. How could you be? You weren't even there.'

He was shaking his head. 'But I should have been. I should have stopped her from driving. I should have come home but I didn't. Even though I knew it was raining hard. And that she hadn't been sleeping. Hadn't been out of the house for weeks. I cut corners like those divers.'

'You did everything you could. You took time off work. You took her to the doctor.'

'I know, but what she wanted, what she needed was time to grieve, time to heal, only I couldn't bear seeing her suffer so I just kept looking for solutions, trying to fix her.'

'You were trying to help her, to look after her because you loved her.' She felt her throat tighten as she thought about her father, about how hard it was to reach someone when they were lost in the shadows.

'I didn't do enough. She was my wife and I was like a bystander.'

'Because it was happening to you too. You were in shock,' she said gently.

'No, you don't understand. I didn't see what was happening.' The pain in his face made her want to cry. 'When the business started to grow, I found it really difficult to fall asleep, so I got some pills to help. She'd been taking them. That's why she'd been so drowsy. I didn't even realise until after the autopsy.'

Her heart lurched at the guilt in his voice. Chase was right. Grief was about time passing but guilt was different. It had to be cut back by someone who knew what they were looking for like a gardener separating bindweed from morning glory.

'People hide things when they're hurting, Chase. And sometimes what they hide hurts them the most, hurts them more than the original pain, whatever that is. But seeing, understanding that is only possible if you're not in pain too. And you were in pain.'

He didn't reply but she felt some of the tension in his body soften.

'I'm sorry,' he said finally. 'You shouldn't have to be dealing with this.'

'It's fine. You needed to talk. I was here.'

His eyes found hers, and he reached up and stroked her face. 'I always felt that telling someone would make it seem like I was wanting to share things, share my life, but it's not like that with you. We have this beautiful understanding of what we are, what this is. Maybe that's why I can talk to you, because you get it. You get that it doesn't change anything.'

It shouldn't hurt so much hearing him describe their relationship like that, but it did. Maybe because it was making her think about her own loss. But her pain was irrelevant right now.

Reaching up, she stroked his face. 'One day, you'll find someone who makes you want to change things.'

He shook his head. 'That part of my life is over. I know what it feels like to love someone and lose them and I will never go through that again.' He slid his hand through her hair. 'Right now, all I want is here with you.'

It was what she wanted too, and it scared her how much she wanted it, wanted him, and she knew that she was at risk of letting it get muddled up with other feelings.

Her pulse stuttered. Who was she trying to kid? It was already muddled. She wanted more than this. More than they had agreed to, and if she didn't act to subdue the way she felt about Chase she would be heading for another emotional disaster.

But she would deal with that later, she thought as he pulled her closer. And, closing her eyes, she arched against him hungrily.

CHAPTER EIGHT

THE NEXT DAY they didn't go back out in the submersible
again. Instead they chilled on the yacht, which was very
easy to do. As well as a swimming pool and a gym, the
Miranda had a steam room, a sauna, a cinema, a bas-
ketball court and, best of all, a library.

Gazing up at the bookshelves, Jemima remembered
her surprise when Chase had mentioned Hemingway at
the bar. There were so many things she had got wrong
about him. Like when he had got so angry with her on
the dive. He was angry because he was scared. For her.
Worried. About her.

She replayed the pain in his voice as he told her about
his wife's accident, and her chest tightened. The thing
she needed to remember was that his concern wasn't
personal to her. Because of what happened, Chase felt
responsible for people, even random divers.

'Pick one. I know you want to.'

Her body stilled. Chase was standing behind her. He
was so close she could feel the heat from his body. His
scent, that impossible to replicate mix of clean skin and

maleness and sandalwood, enveloped her as his arms slid round her waist.

'There's no real order, I'm afraid, but I know the Hemingways are over there on the second shelf.' She could hear the smile in his voice, and she groaned softly. So he had noticed her reaction. Now that she knew him better, it was hard to imagine why she'd thought he had never read a book back then.

'Okay, I may have been a little judgey at the bar,' she admitted. 'It's just that most men I know only read the sports section of the paper.'

She felt his lips find the pulse below her ear. 'And am I like every man you know?' His voice was a hot whisper against her skin.

No, she thought, picturing him that night, how he parted the crowds as he moved. 'You were wearing a baseball cap that first day at the Cycle Shack and then you asked me about fishing so I made an assumption. The wrong assumption. But that's why I was surprised.'

Her heart quivered against her ribs. He was the surprise. Every day, she found out something new, something unexpected, something that made her want to know more, to know everything.

'Pleasantly, I hope.' His warm breath was tickling her skin, teasing her, making her belly clench and unclench, then clench again.

'Of course,' she said hoarsely. 'I like it that you read books.' There was so much more to him than simply thrill seeking, she thought, remembering how carefully he had manoeuvred the sub around the wreck. He was good company too, with views not just on sport as she'd assumed but literature, politics, music.

'That doesn't surprise me in the slightest. You know, I had you down as a teacher when we met at the harbour.'

'Why? Because I was wearing glasses?'

'That, and you used this voice when you spoke to me. Kind of strict and snippy. Pretty sexy actually.'

She laughed. 'You have a one-track mind.'

'Not true.' His voice softened and she felt it like a flame inside her. And she was melting on the inside. It was that easy, that swift. 'I don't just want your body, I want your mind, Dr Friday.'

Something inside her twisted Chase wanting her mind didn't sound like something that should happen in a fling and she wished that Holly were there so that she could ask if he was just flirting. Or if it meant that he wanted more. The possibility of that pulled at a thread inside her so that when she spoke, her voice sounded scratchy and tight.

'I'm not a doctor yet.' And she probably never would be, she thought, her mood dropping a notch as it seemed to do whenever she thought about her life back in England. But that was the downside of a holiday. At some point you had to go back home and face up to all those things you had put on hold.

'It's just a matter of time.'

'And effort,' she said quietly. 'I do have to write it.'

'And you will.' He turned her to face him. 'Are you worried about it?'

Yes, she wanted to say. And not just about her PhD.

She felt overwhelmed and yet also depressingly under-whelmed by her life. Here in Bermuda and with time on her hands, it was easy to see the choices she'd made in the round, and the far-reaching consequences of those choices. How she had stalled somewhere between ad-olescence and adulthood. A student homeowner who dated boys in bands and still borrowed money off her mum.

But after everything Chase had told her last night, she wasn't about to host a public pity party. It would be crass to think his revelations had given her the green light to raise her own woes. That wasn't what this was about. Last night had been the exception, not the rule.

'No, not really. It's just been a bit of a slog. But I should have expected that. I mean, when you have to write upwards of sixty thousand words you're going to hit the occasional stumbling block.'

'But he's not in your life any more.'

'Who?' She stared at him blankly.

'The stumbling block. Your ex.' His lip curled. 'Who is he anyway?'

The directness of his question caught her off balance, mainly because she had, to her astonishment, stopped thinking about Nick. And now that she was having to, it was as if she were remembering him from long ago and far away. He was just a blurred, indistinct shape, almost as if she were standing on the seabed staring up at him through the water.

'He's a singer in a band. He plays the guitar too.'

'Is that your thing?'

Jemima blinked. 'My thing? You mean am I some kind of groupie?'

He shrugged. 'Plenty of women like pouty guys with guitars. That's probably why so many men play them,' he added drily.

'No, that's not what it was about.' She was shaking her head without even realising that she was doing so. 'I didn't even really like his music.'

She felt Chase's narrowed gaze slowly inspect her.

'So why did you date him?'

Because he was a mess, and I thought I could fix him.

For a moment, she imagined saying that sentence out loud but surely that came under the heading of Too Much Information, for a fling anyway. And yet as she looked up, it felt almost as if he knew what she was thinking.

'Was he rich?'

Frowning, she shook her head again. 'The opposite. He was always skint.'

'*Skint?*'

'It means having no money. But it wouldn't have mattered if he was rich. I wouldn't date someone because of their money.' Quite the opposite, in fact. The more impoverished, the more hopeless they were, the better, she thought, thinking about exes. That was what they had in common.

He stared down at her, and there was no reason why she should blush at that moment, but she did anyway.

'So what, then?' She saw him swallow, saw his jaw tighten. 'Is he good-looking?'

Objectively he was, despite what Holly and Ed said.

And yet when she pictured Nick's face, the face she'd once thought so mesmerisingly handsome, she could only see the weak chin and his perpetually sulky expression. 'I thought he was,' she admitted.

The sunlight was behind him so that his face was in shadow. After a moment, he reached out and touched her cheek, lightly. 'You deserve better.'

But I don't, she wanted to tell him. She didn't deserve to find love and happiness.

And yet, she did feel happy. Here. With him.

But of course that was the inherent paradox of the holiday fling. There was this outside-the-lines recklessness to the whole thing that was incredibly exciting and sexy. And because you were on holiday from the usual rigmarole of your day-to-day life you felt calmer, more in control.

Closer.

But a holiday fling was expressly finite. Keyword: holiday.

It didn't matter what happened in the movies, in real life holiday romances came with a built-in expiry date. There was no point in blurring lines between the now and the future. If it worked on the beach, it almost certainly wouldn't work in real life; Holly and Ed had drilled that into her back in England.

And having heard Chase talk about his marriage last night, she had realised something about herself. That whatever it was she had felt for her exes, it was certainly not the kind of love he had described to her. She wasn't sure she knew how to love like that.

Or if she ever would.

She blinked. 'I agree. But I'm not looking for anything serious.' Reaching up, she pulled a book off the shelf. 'Right now I'm happy with Mr Rochester.'

Not as happy as she usually was, she thought an hour later as she shifted position on the sunlounger. That was no reflection on the book. She loved *Jane Eyre*, both the character and the plot. Charlotte Brontë's story of an ordinary woman overcoming the obstacles in her life to find love and lasting happiness with the man she loved was a classic for so many reasons and she had read it countless times, but today she couldn't seem to follow the words.

Telling herself that the sun was too dazzling to read, she shut the book. But it wasn't the sun that was making it difficult to concentrate, it was him.

She glanced over to where Chase lay beside her, his muscular body gleaming in the sunlight. Unlike her, he wasn't attempting to read. Instead, his eyes were closed and she gazed at him greedily, grateful for the opportunity to just stare and stare.

That was what she needed to focus on. His beauty. His skills as a lover. But it was hard not to think about everything he had told her. Everything that had happened to him. Losing his baby. Losing his wife. They were huge life-transforming events and now that she had heard the pain in his voice, she couldn't unhear it. On the contrary, she could feel it reaching out to her.

But she was going to resist it.

Chase Farrar might be the most beautiful man she had ever met, possibly the most damaged. But he wasn't hers to fix for that very reason. She was here for fun, not to dole out therapy, and it didn't matter that she felt so close to him. In fact, that was a reason not to get any closer. Getting closer would increase the risk of him finding out who she was and what she'd done, and she knew how he'd react. Even just thinking about his face changing made her hands shake so much she nearly dropped the book.

No, this needed to stay simple. She needed to sideline everything she was feeling for him, and just embrace the physical need they felt for one another.

They ate lunch on the deck. It was the most perfect of days, she thought, gazing across the deck. The sea stretched away from the boat in every direction, gleaming blue beneath the hazy sun. As for the meal...

Today's menu was the most wonderful food she'd ever eaten. Lobster salad with mango puree and tempura followed by a chocolate and hazelnut eclair with banana ice cream and salted praline.

'Do you like it?'

She glanced up. Chase was watching her, his green gaze resting on her face. He was dressed casually, his feet bare, blond hair still damp from the pool, and just looking at him made her palms itch to touch him.

'It's delicious, but I don't understand how Gianluca does it. How does he come up with these flavour combinations?'

'It's what he's trained to do.' His eyes held hers steady and before she even realised what he was about to do, he reached over and picked up one of the shards of praline and bit into it.

'Hey, hands off.' She pulled her plate closer. 'I was

saving that till last.' But her mouth was pulling at the corners.

'I'm not that patient. I can't wait until the end for the best bits. I want it at the beginning. And also in the middle. Especially when I'm with you,' he added softly.

She laughed. 'Don't try to distract me.' Picking up the last shard of praline, she took a deliberately tiny bite.

He rolled his eyes. 'I bet you're one of those people who unwrap presents really slowly so as not to tear the paper.'

'There's nothing wrong with that. In fact, it's the correct way to do it because then you can reuse it, which is better for the environment. Although personally I'm not a fan of wrapping paper.'

'Really? I thought you'd be all about curling ribbons and tying little bows.'

She held his gaze. 'You'd be surprised at how few things merit a bow. But as it happens I use *furoshiki*, you know, those Japanese fabric wraps.'

He nodded slowly. 'I've heard about those. Can you use any fabric? Like a sheet maybe.'

She frowned. 'I don't see why not.'

His dark green gaze simmered as it met hers. 'Good. Because I can think of nothing I'd like to do more than spend the afternoon in bed, unwrapping you.'

Heart thudding, she stared at him, mute and undone. Impatient. Lost somewhere between the hunger in his eyes and the heat building low in her pelvis.

She cleared her throat. 'Shall we skip coffee?'

He nodded. 'Let's do that.' Leaning forward, he fitted his mouth against hers and kissed her, his hand sliding through her hair, tilting her face so that he could deepen the kiss.

It took both of them a few seconds to register that his phone was ringing. He made a rough sound in his throat and pulled back. Eyes still fixed to her face, he yanked the phone from his pocket, frowning down at the screen. 'I better take this,' he said, getting to his feet and walking towards the pool.

'Would you like me to bring out some tea and coffee, Ms Friday?' Peter, one of the stewards, had come to clear the plates.

She glanced over to where Chase was still on the phone. It was impossible to read his expression, but he seemed to be listening intently, one hand jammed into the pocket of his shorts. 'No, thank you, Peter. I think we're good.' Shifting back in her seat, she stared out across the ocean, which was now a couple of shades darker than the sky. She knew Chase kept in contact with his New York office but he left the day-to-day running of his business to his C-suite. It must be something important for him to pick up.

'Sorry about that.'

He was back. He had only been gone a few minutes but her heart flipped over as he sat down, as golden and beautiful as any of the treasures he brought up from the ocean.

'Everything okay?' she asked, more out of politeness than because she expected him to share the details of his call.

'Everything's good,' he said slowly. His eyes switched to her face. 'That was Marcus. He wanted to let me know that they're just tidying up at the beach house. You can move back in whenever you're ready.'

She stared at him blankly, his words buzzing in her head like a sudden, unexpected swarm of bees. This was always going to happen. Only despite knowing that right from the start she hadn't seen it coming. She'd just let the days bleed into one another beneath the brilliant blue of the sky and got lost in Chase's glittering green gaze.

And now it was over.

'That's great,' she managed. Her voice hardly sounded like hers, but he didn't seem to notice.

'Yeah, he sent photos.' He held out his phone and she took it, and scrolled through the pictures, feeling giddy and faintly sick. 'It looks amazing. Joan will be thrilled. They must have worked really hard to get it all done so quickly.'

'They work fast but they do a good job.' He hesitated. 'So when do you want to be dropped back?'

It was a question that needed answering but her head was still full of how he had just reached across the table and kissed her. Hungrily. Deeply. It was a kiss that made the world tilt sideways and yet it was also a kiss that meant nothing.

Nothing in the sense of feelings and permanence, because this relationship was always going to end when the builders finished at the beach house. Only now that moment was here, it was hard to imagine leaving him. Harder still to picture waking up the next day without Chase beside her.

She felt an ache in her chest but ignored it. That was

what they'd agreed and it was what she wanted, she told herself. There was no point in being disappointed. No point in pretending this was more important than it could ever be.

'Whenever is easiest for you.' She fought to keep her voice light and careless, balling her hands, trying to keep the emotion inside her 'I'll work around your schedule. Are you thinking now or tomorrow?'

'I have that engagement I told you about in New York tomorrow evening.' His face was completely expressionless as he looked across the table, but there was a note in his voice she couldn't place. 'Have you ever been?'

She had forgotten about his trip to New York. Not that it mattered now.

'To New York?' She shook her head. 'No, this is my first time abroad.'

There was a long silence. 'Why not come with me, then? Get your first bite of the Big Apple.'

Jemima stared at him. Was he being serious? It seemed like a step away from the 'just sex' rules of their fling.

'I know that's not what we agreed,' he said as if he'd read her mind. 'But I feel like yesterday things changed. I changed them.' As a gull wheeled across the sky, he glanced upwards, his jaw tightening. 'This is your holiday. I promised you fun, and diving.'

'And you kept your promise,' she protested, and she was shocked to realise that out of all the men in her life, aside from her brother, Chase was the only man ever to do that. 'Lots of people make promises, Chase. Like my exes. They were great at promising all kinds of things. But there's a difference between saying you're going to do something and actually doing it.' Beneath the table, her fingers knotted. 'I've had a lot of fun.'

'Not last night, you didn't. You had to sit and listen to me unpack a load of emotional baggage and I shouldn't have done that. It wasn't fair. You didn't sign up for that. But I thought maybe a trip to New York might go some way to making it up to you. I have this event, but aside from that my time is my own. I could show you around.'

As she pictured the gleaming skyscrapers and the Statue of Liberty, and Chase's hand wrapped around hers, her limbs felt as if they were filling with light.

It was so, so tempting, but... 'You've already done so much for me. You don't need to do that.'

'I want to do it,' he said softly. 'I want to show you where I live.'

She stared at him dazedly. An impromptu trip to New York was the kind of thing couples did. Only they weren't a couple. They were lovers who weren't in love. Friends with benefits who'd only met a week ago and would go back to being strangers when she left Bermuda.

Her nails were cutting into her hands now. The thought of leaving Bermuda, of leaving Chase, made her feel as if she were drowning and, taking a deep breath, she counted to ten inside her head. 'Then yes, I'd love to go to New York with you.'

It was breaking all the rules. But this was her holiday, her rules, she thought defiantly, and she leaned in and kissed him because kissing was so much easier than trying to address any of the conflicting and contradictory emotions squeezing her heart.

At some point she was going to have to say goodbye, but not yet. Not until after New York.

New York. New York. So good they named it twice. Maybe that was why his heart felt as if it were beating at twice its normal rate, Chase thought, gazing down at Central Park from the window of his penthouse triplex apartment.

They had flown up late at night, arriving in darkness and to a flurry of seasonal snowflakes. His gaze drifted back down to the lights below. When he couldn't sleep he often stood here watching the traffic, taking comfort from the fact that he wasn't alone.

But he wasn't alone any more, he thought, glancing over his shoulder to where Jemima lay sleeping, her blonde hair splayed across the pillow, her naked body silvery in the moonlight.

He felt his own body harden, and his pulse gave a betraying twitch.

It wasn't the city that was making his heart beat at twice its normal rate. It was her, because, despite having told Jemima, told *himself*, that this arrangement was just a mutual interlude of pleasure and satisfaction, when he had heard Marcus say that the beach house was ready for her to move back in, he had been so paralysed with panic it had felt as if his spine had turned to ice.

It was understandable, of course. He and Jemima had hardly spent a moment apart since that day when he'd gone to her cabin to confront her, and it had been a long time since he'd spent the night with anyone, much less shared so much of his life.

Including the moment when it had imploded.

His chest tightened. For the best part of a decade he'd held it all together, pushed the grief and chaos and despair to the farthest, deepest parts of his mind. And then Jemima had called him out, demanded a respect that he should have given her automatically, and it had shocked him that he had become a man like that. A man who had to hurt others to hide his own pain.

It had shocked him into speaking. And once he started he couldn't stop, the barriers inside him that had cracked and given way like a dam breaking, releasing a flood of trapped memories.

And it had been hard and painful. Just like when he'd dislocated his shoulder last year during a storm and the *Miranda*'s medic had to rotate the joint until it went back into the socket. But now, although it still ached, it was a different kind of pain. The kind you knew would fade rather than need constant managing.

Was sharing his past the reason why he was finding it hard to imagine Jemima returning to the beach house?

The answer to that question, and to why he responded to her with such intensity, were not something he wanted to examine right now.

And he didn't need to. As he'd told her two days ago, that was the beauty of their relationship. It was about living in the moment. There was no need to give yesterday any more thought than tomorrow.

It was enough that she was here.

Except it wasn't.

The ice in his spine was back. He had told himself that he had invited her to New York on a whim, but the truth was that leaving her behind in Bermuda was not an option. Not when they had so little time together remaining. Now the panic was back too, sliding over his skin smoothly so that he couldn't get a grip of it.

'Chase.'

He turned. Jemima was half sitting up in bed, her eyes drowsy with sleep and something else, something that made hunger ripple through his body in a wave that almost knocked him off his feet.

'Chase.' She said his name again but he was already walking back to the bed and as his mouth found her, she took a quick breath like a gasp. 'I missed you.'

'I missed you too,' he said, pulling her against him, with an urgency that was not just simple desire any longer but a need to hold her close while he still could.

They woke late and ate a leisurely breakfast in bed, watching the sun catch the corners of Manhattan's sky-scrapers.

'What do you think of it?' he said softly as her gaze returned to his face.

'I think it's amazing. I feel like I'm in a film.' Her mouth curved into one of those tiny smiles that made him want to kiss the corners and work his way inwards. 'I don't know how you get any work done though. I think I'd just spend my whole time staring out of the window.'

'I'm used to it.' Leaning forward, he ran his fingers

over the curve of her hip. 'But there are other things I prefer to stare at.'

And touch. Caress. Lick.

His body pulsed its approval of that idea but, behind her, the New York skyline beckoned in the distance. Only that wasn't why she was here. He'd invited her because he had to. Because the idea of returning to New York alone had made him feel as if gravity had stopped working and he were breaking apart. Because he had suddenly realised how much he enjoyed her company.

He stared across the room to the view of the city that had been his home for over a decade now. This apartment had been his home too with his wife. After Frida's death, he'd clawed his way out of the darkness and found purpose through expanding his business and looking for shipwrecks, but at the heart of his life there was a void.

Now for the first time he could see how lonely he'd been.

How lonely he would be without Jemima.

With an effort, he lifted his hand from her hip. 'Right, you need to get dressed because we're going to go sightseeing.'

Their eyes met, hers shining, and then the shine faded. 'I don't really have any warm clothes. Do you think I could borrow a coat?'

'Not necessary.' Still holding her hand, he slid off the bed and led her into the dressing room, watching her face as she stared at the selection of outfits his housekeeper had collected from his PA and which were now hanging from the rails. Beneath them several pairs of glossy leather boots and shoes were arranged neatly on the shelves.

'I can't accept this,' Jemima said, reaching out to touch a glossy white puffy coat. 'Any of these.' Her fingers trembled against a pale blue satin slip dress.

'Really?' He leaned back languidly against the door. 'You're quite welcome to walk down Fifth Avenue in that bikini you were wearing in Bermy but I'm warning you, you'll either get arrested or get frostbite.'

'I'll pay you back.' Her cheeks were pink again and she sounded flustered.

'There's no need. You're my guest and, besides, you being here is helping me. So think of it as a clothing allowance.'

'Me being here is helping you,' she repeated slowly.

'I need a plus one for this event.'

'Is that what I am?' She glanced up at him, her grey eyes wide and soft in the light spilling in through the window.

He thought about all the other plus ones he'd taken to similar events. In one sense, yes, and yet all of those women had been interchangeable. If one wasn't available he simply took another. But he couldn't imagine taking anyone other than Jemima.

As promised, they spent the day sightseeing. Jemima was sweetly excited by all the famous monuments. He watched her eyes widen as they walked towards the Empire State Building, and the decade between them seemed to be, not just about age, but experience. Grief had built an armour between him and the world, but she made him notice things that he took for granted. Like the yellow taxis and the screens in Times Square.

'What's this building?' she asked as they stepped through the revolving door into another huge glass tower.

'It's my office,' he said coolly. 'Hi, Mike,' he greeted the doorman, his heart pounding as he guided her through security to his private elevator.

'If you have some work to do, I can—' she began, but as the lift doors closed he pulled her against him and kissed her fiercely. 'I don't. I brought you here because the only way to truly see the city is from above.' Taking her hand, he led her onto the rooftop towards the helicopter that was squatting there like a dark, metallic insect.

'We're going in a helicopter.' Her voice was a squeak of disbelief.

Nodding, he pulled her closer, wrapping his arms around her as a cold breeze lifted her hair. 'Now aren't you glad you're not wearing a bikini?'

It really was the best way to see any city. At around a thousand feet up in the air, you got the kind of view usually reserved for postcards. As they followed the curve of the Hudson, he pointed out various landmarks. 'That's where we're going tonight,' he said, pointing down to the American Museum of Natural History. She glanced over at him, the smile that had been there a moment earlier faltering. 'Are you sure you want me to come with you?'

'Completely. Look, it's just an exhibition. We don't need to stay long. Just show our faces.'

'Your face, you mean,' she said quietly.

Time was supposed to fly when you were having fun so he must have been having a lot of fun, he thought later as he sat waiting in the open-plan living room for Jemima to get ready. One moment they had been gazing down at the Chrysler Building, the next he was changing into a suit and tie and texting his driver to tell him to bring the car round.

He felt rather than saw movement behind him and, turning, he forgot about the passing of time. Forgot almost to breathe. He was conscious only of the hammering of his heart.

Jemima was standing halfway down the stairs, her hair in some kind of loose chignon. She was wearing a cropped white silk shirt and a silver skirt that shimmered beneath the overhead lights. Her nude painted lips offset the smoky eyeshadow beneath her glasses.

'You look beautiful.'

He glanced at the strip of taut stomach, then wished he hadn't as his body tightened painfully in response. 'What is it?' he said as she bit into her lip.

'I've been trying to get these contacts in only I'm so nervous, my hands are shaking too much.'

'Don't be nervous, and don't worry about wearing contacts.'

Her eyes flicked up to his face. 'I wouldn't wear them either, but I honestly can't see anything.'

He crossed the room and took the stairs two at a time until his eyes were level with hers. 'Keep them on.' But take everything else off, he thought, his gaze dropping to the band of smooth skin. 'I mean it. I like that nobody else gets to see your eyes without them the way I do.'

The pulse at the base of her throat jerked forward and heat rushed through him, his body responding, growing hard, and he kissed her softly on the mouth, then drew back, groaning. 'Okay, I think it's time to leave, otherwise I'm going to have too many reasons to stay.'

CHAPTER NINE

HE WAS GLAD he had returned for the exhibition. It wasn't just that it was interesting, he liked watching Jemima. In fact, that was turning into a whole new distraction for him.

And he liked her company. Her laugh. Her curiosity. Her intelligence. After so many solitary years spent turning his back on anything more than sex with the occasional benefit, Jemima made him feel happy and whole in ways that he had not just forgotten but never experienced. It was both daunting and thrilling.

'So this is something your team found.' They were looking at a heavy gold chain that looked perfect despite having been immersed in water for nearly three hundred years.

'We found it in a wreck off the Bahamas.'

She frowned. 'The Bahamas?'

'I went down to help transport food and water after Hurricane Tana hit three years ago.' He saw that she was staring at him uncertainly, as if she wasn't sure if he was joking or not. 'It's not all about the adrenaline,' he said quietly.

'I know that.' Leaning forward, she touched the tiny Monmouth Rock logo on the explainer next to the glass display case. 'Is that why you support the trust?'

She had noticed. He felt a small prickle of surprise. Not many people bothered to look at the small print, let alone details like business logos. But then Jemima looked closer than most people. Saw more. Cared more.

'They do good work.' The International Marine Conservation Trust was one of many charities Monmouth Rock supported. 'I like that it's a joint initiative with marine archaeologists and biologists.'

They spent about an hour admiring the exhibits. Or rather Jemima did. He went back to admiring her. 'Have you had enough?' he said finally as they drifted slowly back through the gallery. 'Or do you want to go to the after party?'

'There's an after party?' she said, and he could see the excitement in her eyes at such a novelty.

'Not officially, but this is New York, New York, baby. You're in the city that never sleeps.' He sang the words softly then spun her round, dipping her in his arms. 'There's always an after party.'

After the cool serenity of the museum, Le Bomb was packed and deafeningly loud so that you could feel the music move through your body. It reminded him of that first night in the Green Door, and he found himself wishing that he could reset time and start again. Instead, he pulled her against him. If they could just keep dancing then maybe the night would never end.

But it did. Finally at around three o'clock in the morning, he felt her start to flag.

'Let's go home,' he whispered. As they walked through the foyer, he felt Jemima's hand tighten around his arm. 'What is it?'

'There's something wrong with that woman.' He turned. A woman with dark hair was slumped on one of the velvet couches in the foyer. Her friends were patting her back, giggling

Chase stepped closer. 'Is she okay?'

'She's just been sick. She'll be fine.'

'Can she sit up?' Jemima sidestepped past him. Squinting down at her friend uncertainly, one of the women shook her head. 'I don't think so.'

'What's her name?'

'Shannon.'

'Hey, Shannon. Can you hear me?' He watched Jemima crouch down next to her. 'Can you hear me?' As the woman groaned, she turned towards him. 'Can I borrow your jacket? And could you call an ambulance? Her breathing is wrong. I think she has alcohol poisoning.'

They waited until the ambulance arrived. On the ride back to the apartment, Jemima was quiet. Remembering how upset she'd got about the divers, he squeezed her hand. 'She'll be okay.'

But Jemima didn't look okay. She looked pale and her skin looked taut around her eyes and mouth and he knew that she wasn't just thinking about the woman. That it was something to do with whatever it was that she had been holding back.

She nodded. 'Hopefully.'

'Well, she's got a better chance of being okay than if you hadn't been there.'

Her face stilled. 'I saw her earlier. In the bar. I should have done something then.'

'Done what?' He frowned. 'Look, you noticed her, which is more than most people did, and you called the ambulance. You did everything right.'

'You don't know that.' She was shaking her head.

'I know what I saw, Jemima.'

'I'm not talking about tonight,' she said shakily. 'And you don't know what I did.'

Chase was so stunned by her words that he didn't feel the limousine slowing in front of his apartment building.

'Jemima?'

He reached out to touch her, wanting, needing to reassure himself as much as her. What could she have done? But she was already out of the car, walking so fast that he had to run to catch up with her.

They were standing in the lobby. As the lift doors opened, she stepped inside and flattened herself against the side as if he were dangerous. Or she were.

'I don't understand what's happening here.'

It was more than that. He was sideswiped by what Jemima had said in the car, and by the sudden, violent change to the mood of the evening. She had not just withdrawn, she was in full-scale retreat, he thought, watching her eyes do a jerky circuit around the lift.

'You don't need to.' He winced inside, hearing the echo of what he'd said to her on the *Miranda*: that their relationship was just about sex. Only it wasn't true then, and it felt even less true now.

As the doors opened, he stepped aside to let her pass, scared that if he didn't, that if he left first, she would take the lift back down and flee into the night. Because he had seen that look before. That need to hide away with your pain. Although Frida hadn't fled so much as sleepwalked.

But back then he had been a different man. A man who was incapable and unwilling to see what was in front of him. He wasn't that man any more. In large part thanks to the woman he was following into the living room.

'I want to.'

'Well, I don't.'

Her eyes were huge and dark as if he was hurting her just by being there and that hurt more than he could have imagined. Hurt enough that he had to press his feet into the quarter sawn white oak flooring to steady himself.

Behind her, he could see a thin, pale line along the horizon and he knew that if he walked to the window and looked down, the city would look like one of those snow globes they sold for tourists. But up here it felt as though everything were still shaking.

'This was a mistake,' she said hoarsely. 'All of it. It was supposed to be a one-night stand. I should have gone to a hotel. I should never have let you talk me into it.'

'You think I talked you into this?' He was shocked, appalled.

'I wish I had been thinking, but I was busy pretending this was who I am, but it's not.'

He stared at her, his heart ricocheting against his ribs. He couldn't believe that she was the same woman who had reached for him in the moonlight. He could remember the heat in her eyes, that fierce glitter of desire. They had been lovers. Now she was looking at him as if he were her enemy.

No, not her enemy, he thought with a jolt. Her executioner.

'Look, I get that you're upset about what happened in the club. I am too, so maybe it would help to talk about it,' he said, and he was surprised and relieved to hear how calm his voice sounded. But that was what she needed him to be because she was in shock, he just hadn't realised it earlier because she had seemed so cool-headed and efficient.

'I don't want to talk.' She looked away to the far side of the room and he saw a flash of something like fear cross her face. 'I want to go to bed. On my own.' Her voice was edged with hysteria and he could see that she was close to tears. Could almost hear her desperation to escape hammering through her veins as she toed off her shoes and edged towards the stairs. And then she was running up them lightly, disappearing into the darkness. He heard a door slam, the slight click of a lock.

He stared down at her shoes, his heart pounding. He felt suddenly exhausted, and cold, as if the falling snow had leached into his bones. But he couldn't risk going to bed in case she sneaked out as she had before. Only this time there would be no note.

Keeping one eye on the staircase, he made his way to the kitchen. Aside from coffee he wasn't a big fan of hot drinks, but he needed something to bring warmth back to his limbs. He made a pot of tea, remembering as he did so that night on the island when she'd found him watching the storm.

It was nature at its most explosive. Stunning and terrifying, even more so when you were out on the ocean, and yet he was more scared now than he had been that night.

He made his way back into the living room and sat down on the sofa. His eyelids felt heavy and, picking up a cushion, he hugged it closer, letting his body go limp. Except it wasn't a cushion, it was Jemima. His arms tightened and he pulled her against him, her heartbeat washing through him, steadily like waves hitting the shoreline.

His eyes snapped open.

'Jemima.'

The cushion was on the floor but she was standing there at the end of the sofa, still in her shimmering skirt and blouse. In the half-light, her face was pale and blurred at the edges, her pupils, saucer wide. 'I'm sorry for what I said. You didn't talk me into doing anything. I wanted it, wanted you, and I don't think it was a mistake. I just wanted you to know that I didn't mean what I said.'

'I do know...' He hesitated. 'And I know that after everything I told you the other night you have no reason to think I could help.'

She was shaking her head. 'I don't think that.'

'I wouldn't blame you if you did,' he said quietly.

Now that she was here, he was desperate not to scare her away.

And she was scared as well as being upset, he realised suddenly, remembering how her eyes had darted round the room.

His feet braced against the floor.

No questions. No conversation. You don't need to know anything about me and I don't want to know anything about you... I want to get naked with you, now, tonight.

He could hear Jemima's voice in his head, could still feel his reaction; that moment of wordless shock followed by a heart-pounding affirmation. Yes, and yes, and yes again.

And for a light-headed second, part of him wanted to pull her closer, kiss away the ache in her voice, but he couldn't do that, not before he knew what or who had made Jemima both fear and seek the shadows. Not before he knew for certain that he wasn't the reason.

'What scared you?'

She didn't react; it looked as though she wasn't even breathing. He only realised he was the one holding his breath when she sat down on the other sofa.

'This. Having this conversation…' Her voice trailed off and she made a small, helpless gesture. 'I never have. People don't know. I didn't want you to know.'

Her eyes drifted down to where her hands were clenched in her lap.

'But you knew anyway,' she whispered.

'Knew what?'

She was shaking her head. 'Remember that first day we went diving?'

His eyes narrowed. 'I remember that I was irrational and unfair.'

'You told me that I didn't follow, though, and you were right. Maybe not about that dive. But about me. The one time it mattered I didn't follow through. I did the opposite, I gave up. Even though he had nobody else I left him. I left him to die.'

Chase stared at her in silence. His heart felt as if it were trying to break through the bars of his ribcage. Whatever he had been expecting her to say, it wasn't that.

'Left who?' he said finally.

'My father.' She sounded breathless, as if she'd been running and maybe she had. Fleeing from the past, the memories, the pain. It was so hard to keep out of reach. Harder still to turn and face them. He stared at her in silence, remembering how it had felt telling her about Frida. But this was her story, he could only prompt her to tell it.

'How did he die?'

'He got hypothermia. He'd been trying to get into his flat, but he was always losing his key and nobody was there to let him in. The police thought he decided to sleep in the porch.'

She was shaking now as if she was cold too.

'Why didn't he go to a friend's house or a hotel?'

'He didn't have any friends. He didn't have anyone. He had people he drank with, but they were like him.'

'Like him?'

'He was an alcoholic. I don't know exactly when it started but by the time I came along it had gone from him liking a drink to needing one. And then another, and another.'

The exhaustion in her voice came from another time.

'That must have been hard.'

She bit her lip. 'It was. Particularly for my mum. She loved him so much.'

'How did they meet?'

'They worked at the same university. He was a professor of political science but he also wrote columns in various newspapers. He had this beautiful voice. My mum used to call him the "snake charmer" because he could get politicians to say things that nobody else could. When he wasn't drinking he could be sweet and funny but alcohol made him nasty, and he kept losing jobs. They got divorced and a couple of years later my mum got remarried to this really nice man called Adam, and then Holly and Ed were born.'

Which explained why the twins were so different from her, he thought, gazing over at her small, pale face.

'Adam's lovely.' Some of the tension in her voice eased a fraction. 'He's so solid and kind. I think him being like that was one of the reasons why I decided to go and live with my dad. Because I knew Adam would look after everyone. And my dad needed looking after.'

'How old were you?' he said quietly.

'Thirteen, nearly fourteen. It wasn't that I didn't see him. I did. I saw him every weekend but I hated leaving him, and it didn't feel fair for him to be alone.' There was a shake in her voice now. 'And I thought, I actually believed that I understood him better. That I could help him. But it was so hard.'

As she pressed her hand against her mouth, his throat felt so tight it ached even to breathe.

'There was never any food. He kept forgetting to buy it, so I got him to put money aside but when he needed alcohol he'd just take it. Sometimes he'd fall over and hurt himself. One time, he collapsed and he got taken to hospital but he discharged himself. Another time he got mugged and he came home covered in blood, but I didn't want to tell anyone because it felt like I'd be betraying him.'

Chase felt his heart squeeze tight. He understood what it was like to feel both helpless and responsible, but he had been an adult. At thirteen, Jemima was little more than a child.

'Had he been drinking that night?' he said gently.

She nodded. 'He drank every night. I'd lie awake at night worrying about where he could be, terrified something had happened to him, imagining all these awful scenarios. But at the same time I'd dread him coming back. He'd just sit there and cry.' There was a tight twist to the corner of her mouth. 'I was tired and stressed all the time, and I was missing school so that I could look after him.'

He saw her bite down on the inside of her lip. 'And then one of my teachers asked me to stay behind. She told me that they were worried about me. About my grades, and I think I'd been waiting for someone to tell me that because I went home and I packed my stuff. I waited until he got back from the pub and I knew he was safe and then I left.'

Her eyes skidded away towards the window.

'I didn't go and see him for a couple of weeks. I was ashamed and I thought he'd be angry but then one day, about three weeks after I moved out, I was coming back from school and he came out of this pub.'

She was still staring across the room, but she was blinking now, trying to keep the tears back.

'It wasn't one he went to regularly, and I didn't recognise him at first. He looked so thin and his face was all red and blotchy, and he had this terrible cough.'

For years now he had fought to keep his own pain at bay but, listening to Jemima work to get each word out, he wished he could take her distress and make it his burden.

'I was scared that he was going to have a go at me, but he didn't. He asked me about school, and Mum, and he told me that he didn't blame her or me for leaving.' Her voice looped higher. 'He said he'd heard me leave but that he hadn't tried to stop me because he had nothing to make me stay. It was the last time I saw him alive.'

Her face quivered and then she was crying, pressing her hand against her mouth to stifle her sobs. He got to his feet and was beside her in two strides, pulling her against him. He felt her stiffen and then her body seemed to lose shape and he lifted her onto his lap and let her cry against his shoulder.

'I should have stayed with him.

He stroked her face. 'You were a child.'

'I left him.' Tears were spilling down her cheeks. 'He had no one in his life but me, and I knew that, and I still left him.'

'Say you'd stayed? Then what?'

'He'd be alive. I would have been there to let him in.' She cried again then and he held her close. Finally as the sky began to lighten, he got to his feet and carried her upstairs and laid her on the bed, peeled off her clothes and his and then pulled the covers around them both.

She fell asleep almost immediately, curling her body around his just as she had so many times before. Why then did it feel different? Was it the way her head was resting on his chest? Or the jerkiness of her breathing?

His heart contracted. It wasn't anything Jemima was doing. It was him. He was the reason it felt different. Because despite his believing that it wasn't possible for him to love again, the impossible had happened. He had fallen in love with Jemima. Fallen in love with the woman at the harbour who had asked for his help in that ridiculously over-polite tone and then turned to quicksilver in his hands back on his boat. The same woman who had shucked open the hard shell he had built around himself, letting the light in on the darkness he'd held so close for so long.

He breathed out shakily. She had made love not just possible but inescapable, necessary. And now that he knew that, he wanted to tell her how he felt. Tell her that things were different. Roar his love from the Manhattan rooftops. This love that had given his life a meaning it had lost when Frida died. A love that would outlive this holiday. A for-ever kind of love. The kind that needed and deserved to be witnessed and sanctioned.

But having told her that part of his life was over, how could he persuade her that he had changed his mind? More importantly, having agreed that this was a holiday fling, how could he persuade Jemima to change hers?

CHAPTER TEN

Breathing out slowly, Jemima gazed up at the ceiling of the sauna, blinking hard. They had woken late, reaching for each other in the midday sun, and as he'd slid into her body she had been intensely grateful for the heat that rushed through her, a heat that blotted out everything but the pleasures of the flesh, his and hers.

Maybe that was why when he'd suggested that they have a swim and take a sauna she had so readily agreed. But this was a different heat and unfortunately it didn't seem to be offering the same level of oblivion.

It was too late to take back her words, but she doubted she could even have done that at the time. Something had happened when she saw that woman at the club. It had tapped into her memory, pressed against some invisible crack and within seconds, the crack had widened and everything she had tried so hard to hold in had started spilling out, and that was that.

She glanced up through her lashes to where Chase lay on his back at a right angle to her. That he was keeping his distance a little was hardly surprising. It was a lot to deal with, and she still wasn't entirely sure why she had felt so compelled to tell him everything.

Not quite everything. She hadn't told him how much she was dreading the end of their affair or how impossible it would be to live without him.

There was a tiny, almost inaudible beep. 'That's fifteen minutes.' Her pulse jerked forward as his deep voice filled the room.

The sauna was one hundred and eighty metres above ground and it had a triple-glazed high efficiency annealed window that allowed you to stare at the Empire State Building while you relaxed. The fact that she had barely looked at the view said a lot about the man who had just rolled languidly onto his side to face her.

Not just his looks. It was how he had acted in the early hours of this morning. It was fair to say that nothing had ever meant more to her than his calm, measured attention and lack of judgement, except perhaps how he had pulled her into his arms and held her, his body warm and solid against hers.

'You don't have to get into the pool now. I know you can stay in longer than me,' she said quickly.

'No, I'm hot enough.' But as he held the door open for her, he caught her hand.

'Let's skip the pool. I have a better idea.' As she hesitated, he smiled down at her, just a slight, teasing curve of his lips. 'Come with me. I think you'll like it. Here, put this on—' he handed her a robe and some flip-flops '—and these. You can't go in barefoot.'

He led her along the side of the pool and opened a door into what she had assumed was a changing room.

It wasn't. She stared in amazement. It looked almost like the sauna except that, instead of wood, the walls were clad in stone and everything was covered in what looked like…

'Is this snow?'

Shutting the door, he nodded. 'I was doing business in Dubai, and they had one of these in the hotel.'

'This is completely wild. Is this actual snow?' She stared up dazedly at the ceiling, blinking into the tiny white crystals dropping onto her face.

'It snows all day every day if you want it to. Solar power, before you ask, and, while I remember, the jet we flew here on is powered by sustainable fuel.'

She smiled. 'I'm impressed, but I'm also curious as to why you want it to snow every day.'

'It's supposed to be good for you. Mainly though it's because it only snows about twelve days a year in New York and I miss the snow back home.' His green eyes locked onto hers. 'I thought you might be missing it too. Home, not the snow. Or maybe that as well.'

There were snowflakes on the end of his eyelashes. For a moment she couldn't speak; her breath was knotted in her throat.

'Because of last night,' he said softly. He reached over and touched her cheek and it was impossible not to lean into the warmth of his hand. 'Look, I know you probably feel weird, but you don't need to. We both had things we'd been holding onto a long time. I'm just glad to have been of some help.'

For a moment she thought he was going to say something else but then he reached out and took her hands and pulled her against him, his green eyes resting on her face as he rubbed his nose against hers.

'And because we have this trust thing I'm going to let you into a secret. The real reason I have this room is so I can build snow people.'

She felt a tug of heat low down as he caught her smile. And relief that she hadn't wrecked these last days together.

'You should just come to Edale if you want to do that.' Realising the implications of her words, she said quickly, 'We get masses of snow where I live. It's beautiful, like something from *The Snow Queen*.'

His eyes were steady and unblinking on her face. 'Maybe I could drop by next time I'm in London.'

She felt a rush of something that she knew to be happiness, which was ridiculous because another part of her knew that it would never happen. Should never happen, according to the rules of the holiday fling. Only this didn't feel like a fling any more. For either of them.

But then again she knew only too well how attracted she was to the dark and unpredictable and there was no point in trying to ignore that fact or the disastrous consequences of ignoring it.

'It's not exactly drop-by-able but I'd like that,' she said carefully. 'But first I'd really like to go back to Bermuda. To the beach house. I don't feel like I've spent nearly enough time there and it's nearly time for me to go home.' She knew that, of course, but saying it out loud made it suddenly, painfully real. Her heart punched upwards into her throat as she tried to picture the blank space where Chase would have stood, the silence of her world without his voice.

No, not yet.

She took a breath. 'And I'd really like you to come with me.'

He touched her cheek, brushed his thumb over her bottom lip and then tilted her head up to meet his. 'I'd like that too,' he said softly.

It was better that they had talked, Jemima thought as she stared through the window of Chase's private jet at the brilliant blue sky. Aside from inviting him to build snow people in Edale, of course.

It was noticeably easier to breathe and her body felt looser and lighter now, as if a burden had been lifted from her shoulders. And really that was exactly what had happened. Before today, talking about her father, his life, his death had been out of bounds and impassable for so long, like those terrible war zones where landmines were still waiting to be cleared.

It hadn't been painless to say what had to be said, but with Chase's arms wrapped around her the flame had been pure and contained like a votive candle. It was a flame that would never go out, but it would never hurt her any more either.

And now she could see how much of her life had been dictated by her guilt and her grief. How it had cast a shadow over her like a mourning veil. But Chase had lifted the veil, and she had let him because she knew he understood what she was feeling. He had felt it himself, and been as trapped.

With hindsight, it was obvious that they'd had that in common all along, which was no doubt why it had been so easy to leapfrog from one-night stand to holiday fling, and now to this understanding that she had never had with anyone before, not even the twins.

There was still an irrevocable sadness that her father hadn't been able to cope with life without a drink, but she had accepted that dating damaged men would never fix the past. Things felt clearer now, and not just the past.

She could picture the title of her thesis, the chaotic pages of notes, only now patterns were forming, sentences shifting into focus. Blinking into the sunlight, she turned her head, and felt her pulse jerk as she found Chase looking at her as if he'd been waiting for her to turn or perhaps to say something. For a moment, all she could do was gaze at him.

He was so beautiful, but he was so much more than that. He was a good boss and he cared about people, the planet… Her breath caught. He cared about her.

'What is it?' he said softly.

'Could I borrow your laptop? I left mine on the *Miranda*. Would you mind?'

'Of course not. Help yourself.' He handed it to her, and in answer to the curiosity in his green eyes, she said quietly, 'I just need to write a few notes for my thesis.'

She wrote solidly for the remaining two hours of the flight time. Wrote more in those two hours than she had written in the previous six months. It wasn't finished but she had a title that was worthy of the word-count, and a structure.

'Is it going well?'

Looking up, she found Chase watching her again, and she nodded slowly. 'I don't know why but I think I know what I'm doing.'

'Of course you do. You're going to save the world. You've already saved me.'

I have?

The question formed in her mouth but before she had a chance to ask it, his phone buzzed, and as he glanced down at the screen she forgot about what his answer might be. His eyes were suddenly blazing green.

'What is it?'

'It's Billy. The lab results have come back.' There was a shake to his voice. 'That cooking pot they found near that partial wreck off the south-eastern reef, it looks like it might come from the Portuguese fleet that disappeared in 1594.'

She squeezed his hand. 'That's incredible.' But looking up at Chase's face, she felt her chest tighten and her excitement ooze away. She had seen that look so many times in her life. It was the look of an addict getting their fix: Part relief, part panic that it might not be real. Only she had chosen to ignore it because she had wanted him to be different. Because she had wanted their truths to mean something. And they did, but not enough.

It was never enough.

'You must be so pleased.'

He looked up from the screen, his face blank, as if what she had said made no sense, as if he had forgotten she was even there. The thought winded her. But, of course, she could never compete.

'I just needed proof,' he said slowly. 'Now I know it's out there.' Only that wasn't all he needed, she thought, forcing her mouth into what she hoped was a smile. There would always be the next fix, and then the next.

After the apartment, Joan's house felt even more like a doll's house. As Chase had promised, his builders had done a good job. So good, she wished they could come and renovate the cottage.

The next two days were bittersweet.

Outwardly everything was perfect. That first evening, they made love and they talked, sitting on the sand, some part of them always touching the other. He was everything she wanted in the world right there. He made her world complete.

And she allowed herself that one night, but the next morning and with every passing hour she tried to pull back a little. To not take his hand quite so quickly or lean in so eagerly for a kiss because it was going to stop soon enough and she had to wean herself off him because time wouldn't stop. But even if she could stop it, it wouldn't change anything. It wouldn't change all the ways that Chase was wrong for her.

'What's up?'

She glanced up at him, her head still reeling from the impossibility and rightness of that statement.

'Nothing, why?'

They were sitting on the porch watching the tide turn.

'You're frowning.' He reached out and smoothed her forehead. As always, his touch made her shiver inside.

'I just realised I need to check in.' Because tonight was her last night in Bermuda. The thought made everything inside her roll sideways like a boat about to capsize.

'In fact I should probably start packing.' She started to get to her feet. 'It's a really early flight.'

He angled his head back, his green eyes holding her so that she sat back down. 'So leave later.'

'I can't. There's no more flights tomorrow.' She had checked.

'Then why don't I take you?'

For a moment she just stared at him. Maybe she had misunderstood. 'You want to take me back to England?' she said, finally.

His fingers tiptoed over the curve of her hip. 'I have some business in London next week, but I can just go earlier. You could show me your cottage. We could build some snow people in your garden,' he said softly.

A honeyed sweet lightness was spreading through her limbs. Chase in England, in her cottage. She could see him, crouching on the lawn behind the cottage shaping snow, his green eyes dark like the mistletoe that grew around the oak trees.

'I don't want this to end, Jemima, and I don't think you do either.' There was an edge to his voice, like an actor who wasn't quite sure of his lines. 'So why don't we just carry on like this?'

'Like this,' she repeated slowly. 'So it would be

like another holiday.' Although she would have to go to work.

'Why does it have to be a holiday?' His gaze was dark and intent on her face. 'It could be like this every day.'

She stared at him in confusion. 'How could that happen?'

'It's very simple. I love you and I think you love me.'

Jemima stared at him, mute with shock. Her heart had stopped beating. Chase loved her. He loved her. She could feel her world rearranging itself into a place of yearned-for possibilities, a blurring, swirling carousel of lights and bright colours, and it was so beautiful and she wanted it so badly that she could hardly bear to look.

Her heart jerked inside her chest, making her jump.

I love you and I think you love me.

His words rolled queasily around her head. Every man she had ever dated had said a version of that sentence. And at the time they'd thought they meant it, and probably Chase thought he meant it now and maybe he did. Maybe it could work. She loved him and he was amazing in bed, and he was kind. Considerate. Sweet. She thought back to how he had taken her out in the submersible and then to New York. No one had ever done anything like that for her before. He had wanted to make her smile but he had also held her while she cried.

She stopped herself, pinching off the flow of hope.

Of course, he didn't love her. They had met nine days ago. And yes, a lot had happened in that time but it didn't mean any of this flame and hunger would work in real life. She glanced past his shoulder at the shimmering curve of water and the looping sunlight, watching it break into pieces and fly away like petals. In its place she could see the wet streets of England and cold grey reality.

'But I don't. I don't love you,' she lied. 'And I doubt that you love me. It just feels like love because we're here in paradise and it's all so perfect, but this isn't my life.'

'It could be.'

Could it? Her throat tightened. The desire to agree with him, to pull him closer and tell him that he was right was nearly impossible to resist, but the very fact that she could think that way was a reason not to. Wanting something to be true didn't make it so. She had come here to learn that lesson and, thanks to Chase, she had.

'Please don't do this. Please don't make this any harder than it is.'

'You're the one that's making it hard, Jemima. I'm saying it's simple.'

She got to her feet, shaking her head. 'Yes, you're saying it. But saying and doing are two different things.'

His face hardened. 'And I know that. I'm not one of your ex-boyfriends. I'm not your father. You know who I am. You know I'm not going to break my promises. You can trust me and I know I can trust you because you've made me remember the good things about loving someone, not just the risk.'

She thought about the snow room, and the yachts, and she remembered how his eyes had blazed when

Billy had texted him about the bowl. Yes, she knew who he was. She knew he was addicted to the adrenaline rush of diving for treasure. She also knew who she was to him. She was a novelty right now. Like the beach house. And he was excited by the idea of playing with her in the snow in her garden. But Chase was a man who had a room in his penthouse where it snowed three hundred and sixty-five days a year on command. His command. How long before his attention would waver and be drawn to the glittering prizes waiting to be discovered beneath that endless blue ocean?

The idea of those green eyes drifting away made her feel suddenly sick.

'I do know who you are, Chase,' she said quietly. 'You're a billionaire who looks for treasure in his spare time.'

'And that's a problem?' Now he was on his feet. 'You said you didn't care about money. Except you do if there's too much of it.'

'I care about honesty and right now you're not being honest with me or yourself. I saw how you reacted to that text message from Billy.'

'Yeah, I was excited. It was exciting.'

'You weren't excited, Chase, you were transfixed. You didn't even know I was there.'

'That's not true.'

'I know what I saw. And I saw how much it mattered to you.'

'You matter to me.'

'But I won't. As soon as we leave here, it won't feel

the same. It can't because none of this is real, you know that. You just don't want to admit it.'

'I'm real.' He held out his hand. 'We're real, Jemima.'

She stumbled backwards, needing distance between them. If only she could cover her ears too. That way she wouldn't have to listen to his words and be tempted into doing what she always did. What she wanted to do now, which was let herself be talked round.

'No, what we have is special. It's special and unique and I've loved every moment of it but it's like you said before—the reason it's special is because it's not meant to last. It's a world within a world that has nothing to do with real life.'

'Jemima...'

'I'm sorry, but I can't.'

He stared at her for what felt like a lifetime. She could feel herself crumbling inside. She wanted him to stay so badly but she would simply be postponing the agony.

'This was only ever meant to be a one-night stand.'

'And it didn't stay one for a reason.' His voice sounded raw, as if it were scraping over a wound.

'Yes. Sex.'

As his eyes narrowed on her face, her heart felt as if it were going to burst. 'You're a remarkable woman. Smart and sexy and strong and beautiful. And I thought you were brave. But you're a coward.'

'Please, just go.' It hurt to speak, to breathe.

He walked away. Or she assumed he had. She was crying so much she couldn't see. And now, standing alone in paradise, she admitted to herself what she couldn't admit to him. That he was right. She loved him.

Only she had pushed him away. She had pushed him out of paradise.

CHAPTER ELEVEN

GAZING UP FROM the screen of his phone, Chase felt his chest tighten. The sky was changing, growing lighter by the moment. Ten minutes ago it had been the same colour as the lead ballast bars down below in the *Miranda*'s hull. Now it was the same soft grey as Jemima's eyes.

In another hour it would shift and lighten into a faded blue, and by then she would be gone.

Heart pounding, he glanced back down at his phone. He'd lost count of the number of times he'd checked for messages. Enough to know that Jemima had meant what she said at the beach house. And he could hardly blame her, he thought, replaying the moment when he had told her that he had wanted to carry on seeing her.

As if they were teenagers who had just hooked up at a party.

Unable to sit with that cramping sense of loss and cowardice, he got to his feet and walked across the deck. Leaning against the handrail, he gazed down into the shifting blue waves, remembering how she had swum by his side on that first dive, communicating simply with hand signals, every movement synchronised to his.

He loved her then, this beautiful woman who wanted to save the world.

Had been in love with her since that moment when she summoned him to talk to her about hiring a bike in that crisp, precise English voice. But after so many years of not allowing himself to feel anything, he hadn't recognised what he was feeling. Hadn't wanted to recognise it until that night in New York. Holding her close, feeling the rigidity melt from her body, he had felt not trapped, but freed.

And what had he done with that love?

His hands trembled against the railing. He had waited, waited too long, only acting when she began checking in to her flight. And he should have told her earlier, told her better, but instead he had left it to the last moment. And instead of explaining to her how he felt and why, he'd made it sound simply as if he wanted to keep on sleeping with her, tossing in his love almost as an afterthought.

And now she was leaving Bermuda.

Above him, a lone gull was beating towards the ocean and he stared up at it, seeing instead a plane, her plane moving inexorably into the distance, into an unknown future.

He glanced around the silent deck. Only for him, a future without Jemima was no future.

The sound of the alarm was surprisingly loud in the quiet of the beach house. Not that she needed help waking up, Jemima thought, glancing at the flashing numerals on her phone. She had seen every half-hour and hour since she had woken at three o'clock from a dream that had jerked her awake and left her shaking in the darkness. In her dream, the *Miranda* was disappearing from view and she was in the water, holding up her arm, waving and crying, but the yacht kept moving further and further away until she was alone in the vast blue ocean.

And she was alone now. As she gazed round the empty beach house, the absence of Chase was unbearable. He had made her laugh, made her feel sexy and strong. He had held her while she cried and in his arms she had felt herself healing.

Only she had been too scared to admit her love to him. Too scared to admit his love might be real. Now it was too late.

Picking up her phone, she saw a text from her sister.

Can't wait to see you. The new and the old you. The unstoppable Jemima Friday. xxx

Her heart cartwheeled in her chest. She had told herself that she and Chase couldn't survive in real life but now here was Holly telling her that she was unstoppable. And she was. But she wanted Chase there by her side.

She felt her eyes blur with tears. Experience had taught her to assume that she was only capable of loving irreparably damaged men, and so she had simply refused to accept that loving Chase was an option. That he was different and she was different with him. She had held onto her first impressions like a dog with a bone and it didn't matter that she had lost him and pushed him away, she knew that her love for him was never going anywhere.

Except love wasn't a big enough word for the feeling that now overwhelmed her. A feeling that made everything she had ever called love before feel insipid and colourless in comparison because loving Chase was not a feeling. It was an imperative. He was up there with oxygen and water and food and shelter.

Without him she couldn't survive.

Only she had been so scared that it might not work that she had sabotaged it intentionally.

Her phone alarm chimed again, and, looking down at the time on the screen, she felt her pulse quicken. How could it be so late? Her flight was in less than an hour. She swiped onto her list of contacts, and scrolled down, picked a number.

Somewhere on the island, a phone was ringing. Her breath caught as a man's voice answered.

'Sam,' she said quickly. 'It's Jemima. Jemima Friday—you gave me a lift from the airport. I was wondering if you could come and pick me up. I'm in a bit of a hurry.'

Waiting for Sam to arrive was agonising. She couldn't stay still and in the end she had to leave the house and walk up and down the beach to stop herself from screaming. Finally she heard the sound of his car.

She ran back to the house, darting into her bedroom to get her shoes.

The door was open but Sam knocked on it anyway and she felt a rush of relief that he was there.

'I'll be there in two seconds. I know that there's a speed limit on the island but I really need you to drive as fast as you can because I need to get to the harbour.'

'Why do you need to go there?'

She froze, then turned, her heart in her mouth. It wasn't Sam standing in the doorway, but Chase.

Blood was rushing to her head. She felt as if she were floating. 'What are you doing here? I thought you were on the boat.'

'I was. We found a cannon yesterday just before the light went. It's beautiful, hardly a nick on it. They're going back down this morning.'

'Why aren't you with them?'

Chase stared at her, his heart filling his throat.

'Because I didn't want to be there. Not without you.' Beneath her glasses, her grey eyes were wide and stunned. 'I know you don't believe me.' He took a deep breath. 'And I know you don't love me and you think I don't love you and I can understand why you would think that. Why you would think it was just words. But it's not.'

He gritted his teeth against the tears building in his throat. 'After Frida, I was so scared of loving again, that's why I didn't accept what I was feeling. But I love you, Jemima. That's why I want to come to England with you. Why I had to come here today. I don't want to be anywhere you're not and I know I didn't make that clear yesterday. I said too little, and I know it's too late but I'm not your father. I couldn't just let you leave. I had to come after you.'

Jemima felt as if her heart were about to burst. 'It's not late.' She was shaking her head. 'Not for me. Yesterday, I panicked. I've made so many mistakes in my life and I couldn't bear for you to be one of them. I thought that it would be better to remember all this, remember you, like a beautiful dream rather than try and make it real. But then you went and I couldn't breathe.'

They both moved as one, reaching for another, hands touching, gripping, tightening around each other. She felt Chase pull her closer. 'I shouldn't have left.'

Her hands tightened in his shirt. 'I shouldn't have pushed you away. I was just so scared of losing you.'

Leaning forward, he rested his forehead against hers. 'That doesn't make any sense.'

'I know.' She started to laugh, and then, quite suddenly, she was crying.

'We make sense, Jemima. You and me,' he said softly.

She reached up and touched his face. 'Perfect sense.'

Heart pounding with relief and gratitude, he lowered his mouth and kissed her. Finally, they broke apart. 'Why were you going to the harbour?'

Her face softened and he watched with delight as a blush spread across her cheeks. 'I was going to hire a boat so that I could go and look for you.'

He frowned. 'But you don't know where we're diving.'

'I would have found it because you were there, and I wouldn't have stopped until I found you. X marks the spot.' Standing on tiptoe, she brushed her lips against his.

She felt his hand still in her hair. 'You're my treasure.'

'And you're mine,' she whispered. They stood like that for a long time, just holding each other, their hearts beating in time to the waves falling onto the beach behind them. Finally Chase cleared his throat. 'Talking of treasure, I found this yesterday on the dive. Ordinarily I'd give it to a museum but then I thought of a better use for it.'

Jemima stared at the ring with its tiny blinking emerald. She was lost for words.

'I know it's a little tarnished...'

'It's beautiful,' she whispered.

'I was hoping you might wear it on this finger.' She watched him slide the ring onto the third finger of her left hand, her heart beating wildly, terrified to move in case she woke up from what must surely be a dream.

'I know this was supposed to be a one-night stand...' Chase hesitated. Not because he had doubts but because he had none and he wanted to savour that feeling of absolute rightness for just a second longer.

'It was,' Jemima said hoarsely. 'But then it became two nights, and now I don't even know how many it is.'

He nodded. 'I was wondering how you feel about for ever?'

Jemima blinked. 'Are you asking me to marry you?'

His green eyes were clear and unfaltering and as he nodded, she felt a happiness so pure it felt as though she were filling with sunlight.

'Yes.' Her eyes filled with tears. 'Yes, yes, yes…'

He pulled her against him and she felt his breath shudder against her cheek.

'Jemima Farrar,' she whispered. 'It works.'

'Of course.' He looked down into her beautiful grey eyes, feeling at ease with the world, and with himself, and so in love that he found that he was smiling. 'Or I could be Chase Friday if you prefer.'

'Really? Interesting name.'

'Yeah, I've heard you get one Robinson Crusoe joke, so use it wisely.'

She laughed and he started laughing too and then they kissed, holding each other close, then closer still as the sun rose above the beach and the waves fell against the sand.

* * * * *

#4169 THE BABY HIS SECRETARY CARRIES

Bound by a Surrogate Baby

by Dani Collins

Faced with a hostile takeover, tycoon Gio must strengthen his claim on the Casella family company with a fake engagement. He'll never commit to a real one again. Despite his forbidden attraction, his dedicated PA, Molly, is ideal to play his adoring fiancée. The only problem? Molly's pregnant!

#4170 THE ITALIAN'S PREGNANT ENEMY

A Diamond in the Rough

by Maisey Yates

Billionaire Dario's electric night with his mentor's daughter Lyssia was already out-of-bounds. But six weeks later, she drops the bombshell that she's pregnant! Growing up on the streets of Rome, Dario fought for his safety, and he is determined to make his child equally safe. There is just one solution—marrying his enemy!

#4171 WEDDING NIGHT IN THE KING'S BED

by Caitlin Crews

Innocent Helene is unprepared for the wildfire that awakens at the sight of her convenient husband, King Gianluca San Felice. And she is undone by the craving that consumes them on their wedding night. But outside the royal bedchamber, Gianluca remains ice-cold—dare Helene believe their chemistry is enough to bring this powerful ruler to his knees?

#4172 THE BUMP IN THEIR FORBIDDEN REUNION

The Fast Track Billionaires' Club

by Amanda Cinelli

Former race car driver Grayson crashes Izzy's fertility appointment to reveal his late best friend's deceit before it's too late. He always desired Izzy, but their reunion unlocks something primal in Grayson. Knowing she feels it too compels the cynical billionaire to make a scandalous offer: *he'll* give her the family she wants!

#4173 HIS LAST-MINUTE DESERT QUEEN
by Annie West

Determined to save her cousin from an unwanted marriage, Miranda daringly kidnaps the groom-to-be, Sheikh Zamir. She didn't expect him to turn the tables and demand she become his queen instead—and now, he has all the power...

#4174 A VOW TO REDEEM THE GREEK
by Jackie Ashenden

The dying wish of Elena's adoptive father is to be reunited with his estranged son, Atticus. Whatever it takes, she must track down the reclusive billionaire. When she finally finds him, she's completely unprepared for the wildfire raging between them. Or for his father's unexpected demand that they marry!

#4175 AN INNOCENT'S DEAL WITH THE DEVIL
Billion-Dollar Fairy Tales
by Tara Pammi

When Yana Reddy's former stepbrother walks back into her life, his outrageous offer has her playing with fire! Nasir Hadeed will clear all her debts *if* she helps look after his daughter for three months. It's a dangerous deal—she's been burned by him before, and he remains the innocent's greatest temptation...

#4176 PLAYING THE SICILIAN'S GAME OF REVENGE
by Lorraine Hall

When Saverina Parisi discovers her engagement is part of fiancé Teo LaRosa's ruthless vendetta against her family's empire, her hurt is matched only by her need to destroy the same enemy. She'll play along and take pleasure in testing his patience. But Saverina doesn't expect their burning connection to evolve into so much more...

HPCNMRB1223